Will phantoms walk tonight...

Was this evidence? Evidence of what? That a mummy had been there?

There wasn't a whole lot to see. The scrap of cloth was about six inches long and maybe three inches wide. It was yellowish and looked brittle, just as Bonnie had seen that morning.

What she hadn't seen that morning was something sort of bluish-gray on one end of the scrap. What was that? Mold, maybe? Mold from a mummy?

Bonnie stepped quickly backward and was startled when she bumped against someone who must have crept up behind her.

Her heart slammed against her ribs as a voice said, "Bonnie, I've come to take you away."

THE
PHANTOM
FAIR

LAEL LITTKE

Published by
Deseret Book Company
Salt Lake City, Utah

For the two Bonnies who loaned me
some ideas as well as their name

Library of Congress Cataloging-in-Publication Data

Littke, Lael.
    The phantom fair / by Lael Littke.
        p.   cm.
    Summary: Bonnie, a twelve-year-old Mormon girl, hopes that her ideas for the ward Halloween party will get her into the popular girls' club the Bee Theres, but the situation is complicated by a mummy in her backyard.
    ISBN 1-57345-200-9 (pbk.)
    [1. Mummies—Fiction. 2. Halloween—Fiction. 3. Parties—Fiction. 4. Clubs—Fiction. 5. Mormons—Fiction.] I. Title.
PZ7.L719Ph   1996
[Fic]—dc20   96-26246
                                                                  CIP
                                                                   AC

Printed in the United States of America
10 9   8   7   6   5   4   3   2   1

CHAPTER
1

It was definitely a bad hair day.

Bonnie twisted her head from one side to the other, peering into the mirror, trying to spot even one strand of hair to feel good about.

Forget it. Every strand, every *hair*, just lay there, rat-brown and limp. She pushed the whole mop behind her ears, but that didn't do much good.

And was that a zit starting at the side of her nose?

She leaned closer to the mirror.

It couldn't be. Not today!

It was.

How was she going to face the whole congregation at church today looking like that? How could she ever remember the words to the thirteenth Article of Faith with everybody staring at her, giggling and whispering about how awful she looked?

"Bonnie," her mother called from the front of the house. "Bon-NIE? Come on, or we'll be late."

Bonnie swallowed, testing to see if her throat might be sore. Sticking out her tongue, she examined it for some kind of fungus. Anything that would convince Mom to let her stay home from church today. For the rest of her life, actually.

Her throat was clear, her tongue pink and healthy looking.

"Bon-NIE?" Mom called again; then Priscilla yelled, "BONNIE! Are you putting down roots in there?"

Her sister, Priscilla, had never had a bad hair day in her life, or a bad body year, or even a zit that Bonnie knew of. Missy Prissy Perfect was sixteen and lived in a different universe, one where people, especially guy people, turned around to look when she passed by.

Sometimes Bonnie wondered if people turned around to look when *she* passed by, maybe shaking their heads and saying, "Can you believe it?"

"I'll be there in a minute," she yelled. She wished she had time to call her friend Nazli from school. Nazli was good at cheering her up when things got hard. She'd say something like, "If you think things are bad now, wait an hour . . . and they'll be worse."

She was funny and could make Bonnie giggle away her worries.

"BONNIE!" Mom called.

Scuttle the phone call. It was time to do the worst thing of all: put on her shoes.

Shoes? They could serve as flatbed trucks in an emergency. Or lifeboats if your ship sank in the ocean. How could a person grow feet as big as hers in just twelve years?

Sighing, Bonnie put on the shoes. "Bigfoot," she muttered as she headed down the hallway to face the day. She almost tripped over their old dog, Sport, who always seemed to be in the way.

Mom and Priscilla were waiting by the front door.

"*Hurry*, honey," Mom said. "You don't want to be late on the day you graduate from Primary." She smiled as they went out into the bright October sunlight. "I can't believe my baby is old enough to go to Mutual."

Even Priscilla smiled. "You're going to love Beehives," she said as she got into the driver's seat of Mom's car, tucking her long legs with her wee little size six-and-a-half shoes under the steering wheel.

Missy Prissy had her driver's license along with everything else.

Bonnie dragged her size nines into the backseat

and shoved them out of sight under the seat in front of her. Yeah, right. She was going to love Beehives.

The congregation was already singing the opening hymn when Bonnie slunk into the chapel along with Mom and Priscilla. "God speed the right," they sang, as if in reproach for people coming in late. "Like the great and good in story, If we fail, we fail with glory, God speed the right. . . ."

Bonnie avoided looking at her dad, who sat on the stand because he was the bishop's second counselor. She knew Dad wouldn't scowl at her or anything like that, but still she didn't want to look him in the eye right now. Just two weeks before, he'd given a talk in sacrament meeting about showing reverence by being on time for meetings.

Bonnie followed Mom and Priscilla into the pew her brother, Halden, had saved for them.

Halden wasn't as kind as Dad was about not scowling. He frowned at Bonnie now, and she knew she was in for a lecture when they got home. Halden had just turned nineteen and had received a call to the Romania Bucharest Mission. He would be leaving for the Missionary Training Center in the middle of November.

When he'd received his call, Halden had suddenly become perfect. Apparently he figured she

4

should be as perfect as he was, sitting there in his new suit and wimpy dark tie and fresh missionary haircut.

He had come to church at 6:30 A.M., when Dad came for his ward council meeting. He'd said he wanted to study in the library until time for sacrament meeting. He was so perfect he made Bonnie sick.

When Brother Winkler got up to give the opening prayer, Bonnie wondered why she had been sent to such a perfect family. Everybody except her was great-looking and popular.

Everybody except her seemed to have no trouble doing what was right.

Everybody except her was talented.

Everybody except her had decent-sized feet. She looked down at her offending feet.

She couldn't put off any longer thinking the unthinkable. Was the Beehive class going to accept her as one of them? Becca and Carlie and Ducky and Elena and Marybeth and Sunshine? Those girls were all so perfect and all so pretty and they did so many things together. They even had a special club they called the Bee Theres. They met together whenever they needed to discuss problems.

As if they had any.

They weren't going to let her break into their close-knit little group.

Maybe she would flunk out when she went up to the stand to be graduated from Primary and had to recite an Article of Faith. Maybe the bishop would say, "Sorry, Bonnie, you'll have to spend another year in Primary until you learn everything word perfect."

She wouldn't mind that. She liked Primary. It was safe and comforting, and you didn't have to know a whole lot. What would Young Women be like?

She was scared even to think about it.

Brother Winkler finished the prayer, and Bishop Tolman got up to give the announcements and conduct the business.

"Our annual Halloween party, the Phantom Fair, is coming up at the end of the week," he said. "Our energetic Beehive class has prepared a little teaser for us. Girls?"

He stepped back, and the very girls Bonnie had been thinking about hurried to the stand from wherever they'd been sitting with their families and crowded around the microphone at the pulpit. After a little giggling and grinning at one another, they all spoke in unison:

"Come to the Phantom Fair,
The entire ward will be there.
There'll be trunks full of treats,

6

There'll be hot dogs for eats,
And phantoms will fly through the air."

Then Marybeth said, "It's going to be a Trunk-or-Treat party, so decorate your car for Halloween and bring it to the parking lot full of treats to hand out after the spook alley. We'll start with the eats at 6:00 P.M. on Saturday, October 31."

Staying together in a clump, they went back down the stairs and sat, whispering and giggling, on a vacant bench just three rows in front of Bonnie and her family.

Bonnie avoided looking at them.

The bishop took over the mike again. "We want everybody to remember that Halden Olsen's missionary farewell will be on the second Sunday in November. And, speaking of the Olsen family, Bonnie has just turned twelve. Will you please come to the stand, Bonnie?"

Wishing she could float through the air like the phantoms the Bee Theres had mentioned, Bonnie stumbled to her feet and walked up to the pulpit. She imagined Marybeth and Becca and the others whispering about her as she passed. But she didn't look at them to see if they did.

"Would Sister Dunn, our Primary president, and

Sister LeFevre, our Young Women president, come to the stand too, please?" the bishop said.

He put an arm around Bonnie's shoulders when she got to the pulpit and turned her to face the audience. It was worse than she'd imagined, looking at all those faces that were looking back at her, seeing her hair hanging down like old rags and that zit shining like a tiny moon. The deacons grinned at her from the bench in front of the sacrament table—Arvy Dixon and Trent MacAfee and all the others. Guys made her nervous.

"We're very proud of Bonnie," the bishop said. "She has completed all the requirements for graduation from Primary, and she's ready to go on to Young Women. But before I present her certificate, we'll follow tradition and have her repeat whichever Article of Faith she has chosen to share with us today."

Tall as a redwood tree, he looked down at her and adjusted the microphone so she could speak into it. "Which one, Bonnie?"

Why hadn't she chosen number two, which was only three lines long? Why had she thought she had to prove something by doing number thirteen?

She knew why. Because every one of the Beehives—except for Ducky, who had moved to town after she was already twelve—had recited the thirteenth Article of Faith when she graduated from Primary.

Bonnie cleared her throat. "Article of Faith thirteen. We believe . . ." she began. Her voice boomed back at her from the sound system.

She tried again. "We believe . . ."

What came next? What was it we believed?

She stepped closer to the pulpit, and the toes of her atrocious feet hit the side, making a loud thunk.

"We believe . . ." she gasped. She pushed her hair back, trying to think.

" . . . in being honest . . ." the bishop prompted in her ear.

Gratefully she snatched up the words. "We-believe-in-being-honest-true-chaste-benevolent-virtuous-and-in-doing-good-to-all-men," she said in a rush before the words left her again. "Indeed, we may say we follow the admonition of Paul." She felt more confident now. "We believe all things, we hope all things, we have endured many things, and hope to be able to endure all things."

She made the mistake then of looking down at the row of Bee Theres. Their eyes were on her. Were they silently cheering her on, or were they waiting for her to flub the rest so they wouldn't have to take her into their class and especially into their Bee Theres club?

"If there is anything virtuous, lovely, or praisewor-thy . . ." No, that was wrong. She *knew* she'd get the words in the wrong order. "Lovely, or of good report," she corrected, her voice shaking, "or PRAISE-WORTHY . . ." She was so happy to be near the end that she almost blasted the congregation out of their seats with that word.

"Praiseworthy," she said in a softer voice, "we seek after these things."

Her pounding heart almost strangled her. She could feel sweat forming on her forehead, but she'd finished the thirteenth Article of Faith.

"Fine, Bonnie," Bishop Tolman said. "Here's your certificate of graduation."

He handed her a stiff sheet of paper, which she crumpled to her chest. She had to stay there for a couple more minutes while the Primary president told how much they would miss her and the Young Women president said how excited they were to receive her.

Sure. Excited.

Both Sister Dunn and Sister LeFevre hugged her. Her dad and the bishop and the other counselor shook her hand.

Then at last she could escape.

She hurried down the stairs and walked toward her family. She was almost there when she stepped sideways to avoid a small plastic bowl of Cheerios that a mother had brought to keep her child quiet. Those ski-length feet of hers tangled together and she found herself suddenly on the floor.

She heard Halden groan as she looked up into the startled faces of her new classmates, the perfect Bee Theres.

CHAPTER
2

Bonnie closed her eyes. Maybe if she just lay there, the meeting would go on and she could slink out. Or maybe she could crawl underneath a bench. Opening one eye, she looked through the forest of dangling legs under the benches. Two pairs of eyes, belonging to two small children lying on their stomachs, looked back at her. One of the kids whispered, "You spilled my Cheerios."

She closed her eye again. Before she could decide what to do, the Bee Theres, all six of them, rushed out of their seats and knelt beside her.

One of them—it sounded like Sunshine—whispered, "Bonnie! Are you okay?"

"Is she breathing?" That was Marybeth.

"Call the Scouts," Carlie said urgently. "They know how to do CPR."

CPR? Cardiopulmonary resuscitation? The *Scouts?*

Bonnie sat up quickly. "I'm breathing," she said.

Her mother was standing now, reaching for her. "Bonnie," she whispered, "are you hurt? Can you get up?"

"Sure, Mom." She got to her feet while Elena scooped up Cheerios and dumped them back into the plastic bowl.

Bonnie smiled reassuringly at her dad, who stood beside his seat on the stand. Then she mouthed "I'm okay" to the bishop, who was still at the pulpit.

He looked relieved as he nodded to the organist to begin playing the sacrament hymn. "I stand all amazed . . ." the congregation sang.

Hunching over so that maybe not every single person in the whole chapel had to see her, Bonnie slid onto the bench between her mom and Priscilla, who each put an arm around her shoulders. On Priscilla's other side, Bonnie could see Halden staring straight ahead with his hand in front of his mouth. Was he snickering to himself, or was he trying not to barf? Or maybe he was just being perfect.

She couldn't help but notice that all the Bee Theres, three pews in front, glanced back at her as they settled again into their places.

She slid down low on the bench.

Mom patted her hand. "It's all right," she

whispered. "The important thing is that you weren't hurt."

That was a typical mom thing to say. Was there a mom school somewhere that taught mothers to say, "Nobody will notice that zit if you smile," and "Your feet aren't so big; you just haven't got your full growth yet," and "The important thing is that you weren't"?

The important thing was that she'd been a total klutz, and there wasn't another girl in the whole Beehive class who would forget the thirteenth Article of Faith, then trip over her own feet and fall flat on her face.

After the meeting was over, Bonnie slunk down the crowded aisle to the foyer. Maybe she could hurry outside before anybody noticed her; she could hide in the shrubbery until the meetings were over. Or maybe she'd just walk home. It was only about two miles to her house.

But before she could do anything, her old Primary classmates, Lindy and Arabella, came up on either side of her.

"Did you hurt yourself, Bonnie?" Lindy asked.

Bonnie shook her head. Lindy and Arabella were used to her clumsy ways and she knew they were just being sympathetic, not making fun of her. "I'm okay," she said.

Arabella smiled. "Aren't you the lucky one, going upstairs to the Beehive class while we head down the hall with the babies."

Lindy rolled her eyes. "You'll probably be having parties and scavenger hunts and all that stuff with the Scouts and the other guys!"

Lindy was only eleven, but she was already boy crazy.

Bonnie wasn't boy crazy. It wouldn't do her any good. She was taller than all the guys her age and had bigger feet. But who would want to be crazy about Arvy Dixon or Trent MacAfee or any of the other Scouts?

"Maybe I'll come back to our Primary class with you," she said.

Just then their teacher, Sister Drake, came by, her arms laden with visual aids. "We'll miss you, Bonnie," she said, "but you'd better run along or you'll be late on your first day." She turned to Lindy and Arabella. "Let's go, girls. We need to plan the daddy-daughter dinner after we've gone over the lesson."

She hurried off down the hall.

Bonnie watched her go. She wished she could help plan the daddy-daughter dinner. They'd had fun last year when they'd served only foods that started with *d*, like deviled crabcakes and dumplings and deep-dish apple pie.

"Huh!" Lindy said. "*We* have to plan a D.D.D. while *you* get to work on the Phantom Fair with the guys." She and Arabella waved as they followed Sister Drake.

Bonnie had forgotten for a moment about the Halloween party. This was the first year that she would be a haunt*er* rather than a haunt*ee*. She wouldn't be one of the little kids going from car to car at the Trunk-or-Treat party, filling her bag with candy and sweets that would give her a stomachache later. This year she would be one of those who did the haunting in the spook alley.

She turned and started upstairs to the room where the Young Women held their opening exercises. She loved Halloween. It was the only day in the year when it was okay, in fact a real asset, to be a freak.

Pausing at the door of the opening exercise room, she peeked around the frame. If the other girls were whispering about how clumsy she'd been in the chapel, she could still sneak away.

But nobody was there. Had they all gone home because she was coming?

No, she could hear voices from the rooms farther down the hall. She was late. She'd missed whatever the girls did before splitting up for classes.

She recycled her earlier thoughts of hiding in the shrubs.

But then she would miss the plans for the Halloween party.

Tiptoeing down the corridor, she passed a room where the older girls were meeting. The Laurels. They stared at her as she stumbled past the door. Talk about perfect. *Those* girls knew everything.

In the next room Sister Rhoda Jackson stood by the chalkboard. This had to be the right room, because Sister Jackson was the Beehive teacher. She was an older lady who always looked perfect, as if she'd just come out of a beauty parlor. That was a little scary, but Bonnie knew the Beehives liked her.

Sister Jackson was talking about a service project one of the girls had apparently done.

Bonnie leaned around the door frame. To her surprise she saw a big paper banner across the front of the room, anchored with balloons. The banner said, "WELCOME TO THE BEEHIVE CLASS, BONNIE."

It wasn't even a computer-printed banner. Somebody had taken the trouble to do it with poster paints. Bright flowers grew out of the letters, and there were sparkly lines all around her name.

"Wow," Bonnie whispered. "Balloons!"

Sister Jackson and all the girls looked toward the door.

"Oh, Bonnie," Sister Jackson said with a smile. "Come right in. We've been waiting for you."

Bonnie's cheeks flamed. Why had she stood there hanging her head around the door frame like a sneaky-peeky? What a baby thing to do!

She slunk in, catching one of her big feet on the legs of a chair and falling heavily onto it.

"No, sit here, Bonnie," Ducky said. She moved over one chair, leaving the seat between her and Becca vacant.

Several girls patted Bonnie on the back and arms to welcome her as she switched chairs. "We're glad to have you join us," Elena said.

Nobody said anything about what had happened earlier in the chapel.

Nobody snickered about her feet.

They were all smiling at her.

"I'm glad to be here," she said. She was. The girls were nice.

"We thought you'd gotten lost and our banner would be wasted," Marybeth said. "We really slaved away on it yesterday at Sister Jackson's house."

The other girls laughed. Apparently they'd had a good time, slaving away. They'd had a lot of good times, Bonnie knew. They'd gone away to a historical

18

farm together where there'd been a ghost; they'd been in the roadshow together; they'd gone to girls camp; and maybe best of all they'd all been bridesmaids at the wedding of their former teacher, Pamela.

How could she hope to become part of a group that had already shared so much?

"I worked my fingers to the bone on those flowers," Becca said. "See the red ones? That's blood, girl."

Sunshine snorted. "Sure it is. More likely it's ketchup from your Big Mac."

All the girls laughed.

It was a sharing kind of laugh. Bonnie figured they'd probably gone to McDonald's to plan what they were going to do before they went to Sister Jackson's house to make the poster. Everybody knew about their club, called the Bee Theres because they'd pledged to always "be there" for one another. Whenever they had something to discuss, the Bee Theres met at the Golden Arches.

Now it seemed as if she might actually become part of the club. She could almost taste the Big Macs and fries.

Maybe it was going to be fun, after all, to be a Beehive, and especially to be a member of the Bee Theres.

Sister Jackson rapped on the table to get attention. "We're glad to have you in our class, Bonnie," she said. "Welcome to the Beehives." She smiled again, then got more businesslike in her tone. "Now, we must go on. Marybeth, will you take over? We need to get organized for the Phantom Fair since it's coming at the end of this week."

Turning to Bonnie she explained, "We're late starting on this due to stake conference last Sunday."

Marybeth, who was the class president, stood up and said, "We've got to get going on our spook alley room. Who would like to volunteer to be our class chairman to put together some ideas and report at the activity meeting Wednesday night? We want to do something really great because there'll be voting for the best room and the prize is a box of frozen Snickers bars."

"Yum-yum," Becca said.

Bonnie thought about how scary it would be to have the responsibility of being chairman. She reached up to push her hair back from her face and was totally startled when Marybeth said, "Bonnie! Thanks for volunteering. Terrific!"

For a moment Bonnie didn't even realize what Marybeth was talking about. She hadn't volunteered.

All she'd done was to put her hand up to push back her hair. Oh, no—Marybeth had mistaken that for volunteering. Her hands were as klutzy as her feet.

"Good, Bonnie," Ducky said. "I was hoping I wouldn't have to do it. I'm still tired from my campaign."

The others laughed.

Even though the other girls were all in junior high and she was still in the sixth grade at the elementary school, Bonnie knew that Ducky had recently run for seventh-grade class president.

"That's very commendable, Bonnie," Sister Jackson said. "Being our chairman for the party is a wonderful way to get acquainted with the young people from the other classes."

The words thudded into Bonnie's mind. She started to protest, to explain that she hadn't volunteered, that in fact she didn't have the foggiest notion of how to be the chairman of anything.

But then Marybeth said, "We need to meet right away to talk about what our class is going to do."

Oh. Well, that was different. They'd get together at McDonald's and eat and talk and giggle and maybe even get around to setting up some plans for Bonnie to report on at the activity on Wednesday night. What was so scary about that? She'd have an important job to do, and before she knew it, she'd be just another one of the Bee Theres.

21

Then Marybeth said, "Let's meet at my house right after school tomorrow," and the others all agreed.

"Is that all right, Bonnie?" Marybeth asked. "Can you come to my house?"

Bonnie slumped. They weren't going to McDonald's after all. Why not? Were they saying, "You may be a Beehive, Bonnie, but we aren't letting you into the Bee Theres"?

How could she get out of being the chairman? She was sure to be a disaster.

"Bonnie?" Marybeth said.

Bonnie sighed. "I'll be there," she said.

CHAPTER
3

Bonnie barely heard the lesson, something about overcoming opposition. Sister Jackson told a story about a chick trying to hatch. She said it was a struggle for a chick to break the shell of the egg to get out, but that this was necessary for the development of its muscles and respiratory system.

"You wouldn't be doing it a favor by breaking the shell to help it get out," Sister Jackson said. "It would die if it didn't go through that struggle."

Sister Jackson looked around at all the girls. "How does this apply to our own lives?"

Bonnie kept her hands in her lap. She wasn't going to reach up to push her hair back again and have Sister Jackson think she was volunteering an answer. She'd already accidentally volunteered for too much. She was no good, anyway, at answering questions where you had to figure out how you were like a hatching chick.

Besides, she was too busy thinking about what she was going to do about being Beehive chairman for the spook alley at the Phantom Fair.

She wished she could get out of it.

But it would really be lame to start whining now that she didn't want to do it. From what she knew of the older Beehive girls, she figured they didn't like whiners.

Sunshine was answering Sister Jackson's question. She was saying something about becoming stronger through struggling to live up to the standards they'd been taught.

"How is that like the chick in the egg?" Sister Jackson asked.

Nobody answered for a little while, and Bonnie ducked her head when Sister Jackson looked at her. She hoped Sister Jackson wasn't the kind of teacher who called on you even if you didn't raise your hand.

She was relieved when Marybeth put up her hand and said, "Well, your parents protect you and tell you what to do when you're little, but eventually you have to peck your way out of the egg and make your own decisions."

"About what?" Sister Jackson persisted.

24

Bonnie kept her head down, peeking sideways to see what was going on.

This time Ducky raised a hand. "Like whether or not to study," she said. "Like being lazy and just watching TV or really getting down to work."

"Like wearing clothes that are too short or too tight or something just because our friends at school do," Becca said. She shifted on her chair, hitching her skirt down over her knees.

"Like boys," Carlie said, and all the girls giggled. "You know, like whether to date before you're sixteen and stuff like that," Carlie added.

Elena rolled her eyes. "Like we have a choice. Nobody's asked me."

"No?" Carlie said. "Augie Krump would ask you out in a minute if you were sixteen."

"Well, what about Gregory Okinaga?" Elena said to Carlie. "He'll be waiting on *your* doorstep the day *you* turn sixteen."

Carlie blushed and turned to Becca. "Have you told the others about you-know-what from you-know-who?"

"What?" chorused the others. "Who?"

Becca blushed. "I got a letter from Joshua," she admitted.

"Oh, wow," Ducky said. "He's the guy you met

25

when you all went to the old historical farm up in Utah, isn't he?"

Bonnie had heard about that. There'd been a gorgeous older guy, about fourteen, working at the old farm, and although he was very shy, he had liked Becca.

"Girls," Sister Jackson interrupted. "Exciting as this subject may be, you'll have to finish it later. Let's get back to the lesson."

Bonnie was glad to get back to the lesson. Talking about guys made her nervous. Guys didn't like girls with feet as big as hers.

Maybe she would put on her big bear-claw slippers and volunteer to be Bigfoot for the Phantom Fair. She could clump around and scare the little kids.

The thought made her vaguely uneasy, but what else could she suggest when all the classes met together to report what they were going to do?

Bonnie was glad to get home that day. She put on the bear-claw slippers she'd been thinking about in class. They were big and gross and old and grungy, but familiar and comforting. Her dad had bought them for her once on a daddy-daughter date when she'd been worrying about how big her feet were getting to be.

"Big feet mean you're firmly grounded," he'd

26

said, holding up one of his own big feet with its size thirteen shoe. "Let's go buy something worthy of those noble feet."

They'd picked out the bear-claw slippers.

Halden had teased her about them from the beginning, calling them her ferocious, atrocious feet, or sometimes her fraudulent, oddulent footware. Halden liked words.

That was before he'd been called to go on his mission and had become so perfect.

Halden used to be fun.

Halden used to love Halloween and the spook alley parties. He and his buddies always thought of more scary things than anybody else.

Why hadn't she thought of that before? Wouldn't he still remember all those things he and his friends had done? After all, he'd received his mission call only a few weeks ago. Those things couldn't have faded from his mind already, even though a person would think now that he'd grown up with a halo glowing around his head.

Bonnie waited until dinnertime to say anything to him. The family always ate Sunday dinner together around the old oak table in the dining alcove, and they always tried to talk about something fun as they ate. Mom wouldn't let anybody bring up problems during Sunday dinner because she said all that did was give people indigestion. "Stomachaches don't come from cakes," she would say. "They come from trouble talk."

But Halloween wasn't a problem, really, or at least it wasn't a problem to anybody except Bonnie.

"Halden," Bonnie said when they were all seated at the table and Halden had said the blessing. "Remember that year when you and Earl and Kevin had your Ghastly Grossery at the spook alley for the Phantom Fair?"

Halden frowned. "What made you think of that now?" He looked as if he might be having a hard time shifting his thoughts from the prayer he'd just said to grim and gross stuff.

"I'm going to be helping to plan the spook alley this year," Bonnie said. "I'm the chairperson from the Beehive class."

Halden looked surprised. "They usually pick the most with-it person in the class to work on the spook alley. How come you're doing it?"

"Halden!" Mom said, and Priscilla muttered, "Really going to make a lot of converts that way, Hal buddy." Turning to Bonnie, she said, "Way to go, Bon-Bon. You must have really impressed the other girls for them to pick you. Didn't I tell you Beehives would be fun?"

Bonnie wished she could blurt out the truth

28

about the way she had been selected. But she didn't want to admit she'd been such a klutz that she had involuntarily volunteered.

Instead, she curled her toes inside her big bear-claw slippers and said, "I know I couldn't do anything as great as your Grossery, Halden, but maybe I could get some ideas if you'd remind me of what you did."

Halden shook his head. "'When I was a child, I spake as a child,'" he said, "'I understood as a child, I thought as a child: but when I became a man, I put away childish things.' That's from First Corinthians, thirteenth chapter, eleventh verse."

Bonnie was puzzled. "So?"

"So he's not going to tell you," Priscilla said.

He was being Elder Perfect again, Bonnie decided.

"I could tell you a few things they used to do," Priscilla said.

Mom looked worried. "Are you sure this is something we should discuss at the dinner table?"

But Dad was grinning. "It's all in fun, Mona," he said. "Besides, the bishop is anxious to make the Phantom Fair something that will attract *all* the neighborhood kids so they'll come to a nice, safe party in our church and parking lot rather than going trick-or-treating door-to-door. That's not very safe anymore."

Bonnie knew that Dad liked Halloween too.

Now Halden was grinning. "Earl and Kevin and I set a really high standard of grossness," he said. "Priscilla doesn't even know some of the things we thought up, so she can't tell you."

"So will you?" Bonnie asked.

"I'll have to think about it." Halden stood up. "Right now I have to go to a fireside. But if I decide to tell you, Bon, you'll have to promise to uphold the honor of the family by doing something equally as gross."

Bonnie felt uneasy again. People were expecting too much of her. The Beehive class, her family, and even the bishop were expecting her and the others to come up with a great party.

She was in a really hard place and was going to have to peck her way out like that baby chick Sister Jackson had been talking about.

CHAPTER
4

Bonnie had strange dreams that night. At first she dreamed she had fangs like the ones Brother Allen and his family always wore at the Halloween parties. Her tongue explored them, feeling their sharpness, and the thought came to her that she'd have to be careful around the little kids at the party so she wouldn't bite them.

Then the dream changed and she *was* a little kid, fearfully approaching a huge black door on which hung a skeleton. She knew some kind of treat awaited her behind that door, but was it worth trying to get past that collection of bones? Shuddering, she turned away and ran.

Suddenly she was herself again, knocking on another door. There wasn't a skeleton on this one, but there was a sign that said in big letters, "BEE

31

THERES." Underneath that, in smaller letters, it said, "Stay out."

That's when she woke up. Her heart pounded.

Did the dream mean anything? Did it mean she didn't have what it took to be on the committee for the Phantom Fair? That she didn't have the imagination to suggest anything the other kids would like? And how about the part with the Bee Theres door— did it mean she might as well forget about ever becoming a part of that group?

She decided to ask Nazli about the dream when she got to school. Nazli wasn't a member of the Church, but she was maybe Bonnie's best friend. She believed in reincarnation and stuff like that. In fact, she claimed that in one of her past lives she had been Cleopatra, and she wore her black hair long and straight like the drawings of that ancient Egyptian queen.

Nazli also claimed that she could "see beyond" and interpret dreams.

She was definitely the right person to talk to.

Bonnie hurried to get dressed in her blue-denim overalls and a short-sleeved, blue-striped blouse. She liked to wear the overalls because she felt that the details on the front kept people from looking down at her big feet.

It was harder to pick what shoes to wear. The

brown penny loafers looked the best on her feet, but her ratty tennis shoes were more comfortable.

She settled on the loafers. She was going to be asking around about Halloween ideas that day, and she didn't want people concentrating on her feet.

Outside she heard Dad's car start, which meant he was off to his job as a teacher at the high school. Priscilla would be riding with him. Mom would have gone already to her three-day-a-week job at the hospital where she was a nurse. And Halden always left early because he was working two jobs to earn more money for his mission.

She'd be alone in the house, so she could slop around in her big bear-claw slippers until she left for school.

But Halden was still in the kitchen when she got there.

"I thought you'd never get up," he complained. "I waited because I decided to tell you some of the great stuff Earl and Kevin and I used to do for our Ghastly Grossery." He glanced down at her feet. "Bon, are you going to *live* in those monstrosities the rest of your life?"

"Thanks for waiting, Halden." Bonnie sat down and poured Korn Krispies into the bowl Mom had left on the table for her. Normally she would have snapped back something about his monstrosity

33

remark, but then there'd be an argument and he probably wouldn't tell her what she wanted to know.

"What were some of things you had in your Grossery?" she asked.

"Well," Halden said, reaching over to pick a Korn Krispy from her bowl, "do you remember the free samples of Dracula's Drink-It-If-You-Dare?"

Bonnie nodded. "I remember." It was just tomato juice, but in dim light it could look like blood. It scared the littler kids, but the bigger kids loved to be cool and scarf it down, then gag and clutch their throats.

Halden munched the Korn Krispy he'd taken. "We had jars of Spook Soup that looked like they had ghosts swimming inside."

Bonnie nodded again. She remembered the Spook Soup. The "ghosts" were just Kleenex tissues.

"And the Broiled Bug Bites," Halden went on, "and the Finger Sandwiches and the Wormy Waffles and all that."

How was she going to remember all these things? She ought to be writing them down. Too bad her brain didn't have a "save" feature like a computer so that she could just hit a key and bring everything back when she wanted it.

"Those are great, Halden. Thanks for telling me."

Bonnie pushed her cereal bowl aside. For some reason she'd lost her appetite.

Halden wasn't finished. "How about our Eyesberg Lettuce? You draw eyes on green grapes with a felt pen, then stick them a little bit under the leaves of a head of lettuce, like they're peeking out. Really effective."

Picking up Bonnie's rejected bowl, he poured the contents into his mouth. Elder Perfect was disappearing fast.

As he munched, Halden said, "One last thing. You cook some spaghetti and sort of mound it up and call it your Bargain Brains."

He put down the empty bowl and headed for the door. "That's all I can tell you. Don't ask me any more stuff."

He left.

He probably figured talking any more about the Grossery would make blotches on that halo that he'd been polishing ever since he got his mission call.

Bonnie sat there staring at her empty bowl. What was the matter with her? She should be thrilled that he'd shared all those things he and Earl and Kevin used to do. Certainly it would impress the other girls if she had all those suggestions.

But it all made her uneasy. It made her think again of her dream about being a little kid and

35

standing nervously at the door with the skeleton hanging on it.

Standing up, she stepped out of her comforting bear-claw slippers into her ski-length loafers and started off to school.

Nazli was waiting for her by the bougainvillea bush at the entrance to their school. She was wearing a long, gold skirt and a black top with gold trim. She and Sunshine would probably get along well together because they both loved to wear weird clothes.

"You didn't sleep last night," Nazli said.

Bonnie stopped. Sometimes Nazli made her feel creepy, the way she could tell things about a person. "How did you know?"

"Shows," Nazli said. "Your face is drooping down to your knees. What's up?" She peered at Bonnie with her Cleopatra eyes.

Nazli's mother let her use eye shadow, which made her eyes look deep and mysterious, as if she really did "see beyond," the way she claimed to.

"Halloween," Bonnie said. "That's what's up."

Nazli grinned. "That's nothing to droop about. What's the problem?"

Bonnie motioned for Nazli to sit with her at the edge of the stairs, partially hidden from the other kids by the bougainvillea.

"I've got a lot to tell you," she said. Forget the

dream. She needed to discuss bigger stuff. She looked around to make sure nobody was near. She preferred not to have anybody hear what she had to say.

She told Nazli all about being appointed to be the Beehive class spook alley chairman, and about how worried she was about it. Nazli knew about the parties because Bonnie had talked about them in past years, but she hadn't ever come to one.

"And so," Bonnie finished, "I want to do something really great. Something that will make the other kids think I'm not so bad after all."

Nazli raised her penciled eyebrows. "You *aren't* so bad after all, Bon. What makes you think you are?"

There wasn't time to go into all that.

"I just want to make a good impression," Bonnie said. "Then maybe the other Beehives will let me join their club. You know. I've told you about that. The Bee Theres."

Nazli squinted at her. "Why is it so important to be let into the Bee Theres?"

What did she mean, why was it important? Bonnie had told her at least two weeks ago about how much she was looking forward to turning twelve. That was back when she'd still hoped she would just automatically become a Bee There when she went into the

Beehive class. She couldn't believe now that she'd been so dumb.

"It's important because . . ." Hmmm. She had never really thought about *why*. "Well, because they have fun and tell secrets and they're always *there* for each other."

Nazli gazed silently at her.

"And—" Bonnie stopped suddenly and turned her head to listen. She thought she'd heard a rustle in the bushes behind them.

She couldn't see anybody. Probably it had been a bird.

"And?" Nazli prompted.

"And if I *don't* get in, it means I'm just a nobody."

There. That was the real reason, Bonnie realized. It would mean she was hopeless, that she'd never be popular in her ward or even be accepted by those who *were* popular. She'd always be an outcast, clumping around the outside of the circle with her big, horrendous feet.

Nazli put a hand on her arm. "Listen, Bonnie. When I was Cleopatra I learned that if somebody doesn't like you, it doesn't matter, because there are a lot of other people who do."

"When you were Cleopatra," Bonnie said, "you were a queen. If people didn't like you, you'd just get rid of them."

"Off with their heads," Nazli declared.

They giggled together.

"Want to off a few Bee There heads?" Nazli asked.

Bonnie stood up, brushing leaves off her jeans. "I just want them to be my friends."

Nazli stood too. "I'm your friend, Bonnie."

"I know." Bonnie gave her a quick hug. It was time to go to class. "So, Friend, do you have any ideas for things I can suggest for the party?"

Nazli gazed up at the mountains behind the school. "We'll get a mummy. With a sarcophagus. Bet you've never had anything like that at your parties before."

A mummy? Nazli was right. Nobody had ever had a mummy.

"Not a real one," Bonnie said. "You mean a fake one, don't you?"

"Why not a real one?"

Bonnie felt her eyebrows climbing her forehead. "Where are you going to get a real mummy?"

"Easy, Bon," Nazli said. "Some of them were my friends when I was Cleopatra. They'll come if I call them from their slumbers. They're Egyptian. They're my people. I was their queen."

"Come on, Nazli," Bonnie said. "How can you call them from their slumbers?"

Nazli smiled mysteriously. "Ancient Egyptian secret."

That was too much for Bonnie. "Let's go to class, Cleopatra," she said, picking up her books. She liked the idea of the mummy. It didn't seem quite as gross as the stuff Halden was talking about.

"You know what?" Nazli said, brushing off her gold skirt. "You might know some of the mummies too. Sometimes I have the feeling that you were one of my handmaidens when I was Cleopatra."

"Maybe *I* was Cleopatra and you were a hand-maiden," Bonnie said.

Nazli shook her head. "Not a chance."

"Hey, why not?" Bonnie protested. "I have queenly feet, if you count big."

"You don't have black hair and Cleopatra eyes," Nazli said smugly.

This was what friendship was like, Bonnie thought: having someone who was easy to talk to and to tease back and forth with. So why did she need the Bee Theres? She felt disloyal at the thought that came to her—that Nazli was just as much an outcast as she was. Nazli with her heavy eye shadow and her claim of being Cleopatra and all her weird talk about how she could "see beyond."

She certainly wasn't one of the popular kids, at school or anywhere else.

Bonnie shoved the thought aside. She *liked* Nazli and would always be her friend.

But she still needed to be a Bee There. Those girls—Becca and Carlie and Ducky and Elena and Marybeth and Sunshine—they were *her* people, like the Egyptians were Nazli's people. She wanted them to like her.

As they started into the school, Bonnie heard a rustling again. Turning quickly, she peered into the bushes.

Someone was in there. Someone who had heard every word she and Nazli had said.

CHAPTER
5

During math class Bonnie worried about the mysterious rustling in the bushes. Why had the person been there? No one could have known that she and Nazli were going to sit down there to talk, so it wasn't as if anyone could have been spying.

So what was the harm if whoever it was had heard what she and Nazli had said? They hadn't told any secrets or said anything that would hurt anybody.

She put it out of her mind. There were more urgent things to think about, like how she was going to present all the stuff she'd learned from Halden and Nazli to her Beehive classmates that afternoon. Should she tell it all to them? Would they be grossed out the way she'd been?

First she needed to find out how much they wanted to do. Maybe they wouldn't even want to go all out on something like Halden's Grossery. Maybe it would be better just to concentrate on something really great and different, like the mummy.

Especially if Nazli could get a real one.

But weren't all mummies in museums? They weren't likely to rent one out for a dumb Phantom Fair. And even Nazli's own people wouldn't send one all the way from Egypt, whether or not they'd been Cleopatra's friends.

For a moment Bonnie thought of Egypt. Ancient, mysterious Egypt with its pharaohs and pyramids and all that.

Maybe it *could* happen.

On the other hand, if Nazli couldn't get a real mummy, they could make their own. The sixth grade had just completed a unit on Egypt and had designed sarcophagus lids.

"Bonnie? Bonnie Olsen? Are you there, Bonnie?"

Bonnie slowly became aware that Mr. Blake, her math teacher, was talking to her.

"Bonnie," he said, "could you give me just a *fraction* of your attention?"

The other kids giggled.

Fraction. They were doing a unit on fractions that week. Mr. Blake liked to make puns.

"I'm sorry." Bonnie felt her cheeks redden. Her thoughts had been so far away that she'd forgotten

43

she was in a classroom. Should she tell them she'd been thinking about mummies? No, now that Mr. Blake had started off on puns, somebody was sure to say, "Well, what about daddies?" Then they'd all snicker and think she was a real nut case.

So she didn't explain.

Mr. Blake was kind. "It's all right, Bonnie. Now that you're back with us, listen to the problem again."

It was one of those complicated problems involving measurements. You had to figure out what fraction of a yard two feet were, then add that to some other fractions and change the result into whole numbers. She was sure somebody was going to make puns about her own big feet. But no one said anything, and Bonnie solved the problem easily enough, now that she was concentrating.

From the other side of the room, Trent MacAfee grinned at her. Trent was in the Scout troop at church, and sometimes she'd seen him teasing the Beehive girls with the other guys, singing, "Buzzy, buzzy Beehives, looking for their honey."

So why was he grinning at her now? Had she done something goofy?

Was Trent the one who'd been hiding in the bushes outside? Was that why he was grinning?

She stared back at him. His ears reddened, and he looked away.

None of the other girls were there when Bonnie arrived at Marybeth's for the meeting after school. She was afraid for a moment that she'd gotten the time wrong, or the day. But Marybeth smiled and invited her in, saying, "The others will be along in a few minutes. They stayed at school to help Ducky with a project."

She led Bonnie into the family room. "Let's just sit here and talk until they come," she said, "then we'll go upstairs to my room."

Bonnie was uncomfortable. What could she say to Marybeth? Marybeth was the most perfect of all the Bee Theres, with her big house and pretty face and long hair and little feet.

But it didn't matter, after all, because Marybeth did the talking.

"I'm glad you came into our class before I leave," she said, "so that I could get to know you."

That puzzled Bonnie. She hadn't heard anything about Marybeth going anywhere. "Are you moving?" she asked.

Marybeth smiled. "No. It won't be too long until I'm fourteen and go into the Mia Maid class."

Bonnie felt embarrassed. She should have known that Marybeth was talking about leaving the class, not leaving town.

It made her sad to think about it. She'd really been a dork for not realizing that the Beehive class and the Bee Theres would not go on forever. She'd been thinking that if she could just get into the Bee Theres she'd have reached eternal happiness. Why hadn't she realized that the way things were right now was only temporary?

An awful thought came into her mind. Would all the other girls be going into the Mia Maid class too? Would she be the only Beehive left? It would be a while before Lindy and Arabella would be old enough to come into Young Women.

"Are any of the others going to turn fourteen soon?" she asked.

"Not for several months," Marybeth said. "The next one will be Becca. Then Elena."

Oh, no. Would there even be a Bee Theres club when Marybeth and Becca and Elena were advanced to the next class? Was she going to miss it all?

She wished she could freeze time right at this moment, so that things would remain the same for a long, long time. Like the mummies Nazli had talked about. They had been preserved just as they were for centuries. You didn't have to worry about a mummy going on to become something else just because it turned a year older.

She was still worrying about the changes ahead

when Carlie, Becca, Ducky, Sunshine, and Elena arrived.

"Hi, Bon," they all said, and for a moment Bonnie was happy. Giving her a nickname seemed to be a good sign.

"Let's go up to my room," Marybeth said, "and get this meeting going."

That made Bonnie happy too. She'd heard about Marybeth's fabulous room from Priscilla, who was a good friend of one of Marybeth's older sisters. She'd heard about its purple carpet and jewel-tone bedspread, which all seemed to fit with Marybeth's dark brown hair and vivid complexion.

When they got there, Bonnie saw it was as pretty as she'd expected. The four-poster bed was even made, something Bonnie frequently didn't do in the morning when she was rushing to get to school.

Maybe Marybeth's family had a maid who did it.

Dark curtains at the windows kept out a lot of the sunlight and gave the room the appearance of a plush cave. It was fabulous. There were shelves along one wall that held about fifty teddy bears. They made the pretty room cozy.

It was tidy, too, with books and clothes all put away where they belonged. Bonnie vowed that if the group ever came to her house, she would never let them see her messy, cluttered room with its painted, secondhand furniture and unmade bed. She had a pretty spread that looked like an old quilt, but she seldom pulled it up over the rumpled blanket and sheets.

"Sit down," Marybeth said, and the girls plopped down wherever they were, some on the bed, some on the floor. Bonnie sat on the floor with her back against the desk. Being allowed to be here in Marybeth's room was almost as good as going to McDonald's, especially when Marybeth pulled a tall can of popcorn from under the desk and told everybody to eat.

"So," Marybeth said as soon as everyone was munching, "let's get on to the business. I've got some ideas for our room for the spook alley, and Carlie told me at school that she had some too."

Bonnie looked around the group. After all her worrying about gathering ideas, wasn't she going to have a chance to share them? Had they forgotten she was the chairman? Or didn't they trust her to think up anything good?

"Carlie," Marybeth said, "you report first. And Bonnie, there are pencils and paper in the top drawer of the desk, if you want to write down the things we talk about so you'll have some different choices you can report on at the meeting."

Bonnie shifted around to pull out a pencil and

48

pad. Okay. It was still up to her. She wasn't sure whether she was glad or sad. She hadn't wanted the job. On the other hand, now that she was into it, she thought she'd like to see it through to the end.

"Well," Carlie said. She was sitting on the bed, and she leaned forward as she spoke. "I was thinking we might have a graveyard with cardboard tombstones that say things like, 'Here lies Samantha Tucket; Tripped over a mop and kicked the bucket.'"

Bonnie joined the other girls in the laughter. It would be kind of fun to have a bunch of funny tombstones that would make people laugh.

But would the little kids understand what was funny? Wouldn't they just be scared by the tombstones? Wasn't the party, after all, for the younger kids? Should she ask?

No, she would just listen, for now. Besides, wouldn't the little kids be scared by *all* the ideas she'd gathered herself?

"My idea," Marybeth said, "was to have a Ghastly Grossery like your brother and his friends used to have, Bonnie. They probably figure they're too old for stuff like that now, since they're all going on missions, so maybe they'd let us use the idea."

Bonnie felt let down. She'd worried about whether Halden would even tell her what they used to do; then she'd worried about whether the Bee

Theres would like a creepy idea like that. And now Marybeth had beaten her to it.

"Eeeee-yu," the other girls said together, and Elena said, "I especially loved the Eyes-berg Lettuce. Write that down, Bonnie."

Dutifully Bonnie scribbled it on the pad, even though it was one of the things she remembered from what Halden told her.

While she was still writing, Marybeth said, "Anybody else have an idea?"

"I'm sure Bonnie does," Sunshine said. She was sitting next to Bonnie on the floor, and she turned to her now. "You must have a lot of ideas, since you volunteered to be our chairman."

Should she tell them now that she hadn't exactly "volunteered"?

No, now wasn't the time for that.

"Yes, I have an idea," Bonnie said. "I have a friend who says she can get a mummy for us. You know—we could do an Egyptian room, with a sarcophagus and the mummy. Maybe make something to look like a tomb," she added when nobody said anything.

"Would that friend be Nazli?" Carlie asked.

Bonnie remembered that Carlie and Becca had been at the same school she attended before they went on to junior high. Sure, they would know Nazli. Everybody knew goofy Nazli.

"It's just an idea," Bonnie said, hating the way she sounded so apologetic.

"It's a *good* idea," Ducky said. "Has anybody ever done anything like that before?" She looked around the room at each of the other girls.

Silently they all shook their heads.

"Are you friends with Nazli?" Carlie asked.

"Well," Bonnie began, then stopped. She'd been going to say, "Not exactly *friends*." But then she remembered how Nazli had said she would always be Bonnie's friend.

"Yes," she said. "I *am* friends with her."

"I like the idea," Ducky said. "It's different."

"Sure it is," Becca said, "but how's Nazli going to get a mummy? I remember she was always talking about how she used to be Cleopatra. Can we depend on her to actually come through with anything?"

Ducky shrugged. "Who knows? Why don't we have Bonnie investigate the idea further and report back?"

The other girls agreed, although they didn't seem very enthusiastic. Bonnie couldn't tell whether it was because they didn't like the idea or because they didn't trust Nazli. She didn't tell them about some of the mummies being friends of Nazli's from the time when she was Cleopatra.

"Okay with you, Bon?" Marybeth asked.

51

"Yes," Bonnie mumbled.

"Great," Marybeth said. She reached over to slap her hand on the desk. "Meeting adjourned. Now, let's get on to the really important stuff. What are you going to wear to the noontime Fifties Sock Hop next week at school?"

After dinner that night, after the family home evening lesson and the games her family liked to play, Bonnie called Nazli to ask if she had located a mummy yet. She kept her voice low because she didn't want her family to hear. Halden would certainly have something to say about calling up a mummy.

He was always saying how dangerous Ouija boards and things like that were, and he might think calling up a mummy was in the same category.

"I haven't located one yet," Nazli said. "I'll keep trying."

"The other girls like the idea of a mummy," Bonnie whispered. "It would be different. I don't think anybody has done it at one of our parties before."

"Maybe I should call up two," Nazli suggested.

"One will be enough." Bonnie couldn't help but think that if Nazli started calling up more than one mummy, they might have mummies running around all over the church.

"Okay," Nazli said. "It's going to be fun."

Bonnie hoped so.

After she hung up, she went up to her room to study for a while. Things were going to work out, she decided.

Before going to bed, she opened a window to let in a little air. It was still summer weather, even though it was October.

The moon was bright outside. As Bonnie turned away from the window, something caught her eye. Somebody—or some*thing*—was standing under a tree in the backyard. When she turned back, she saw it beckon to her before it disappeared into the darkness.

What it looked like was a mummy.

CHAPTER
6

Bonnie woke up the next morning thinking about the mummy. She had awakened during the night, remembering how it had looked, its winding cloths unraveling and its eye sockets huge and black. It had just stood there under the tree, looking at the house. Looking at her. And beckoning.

The memory had made her shiver. She'd pulled her quilt up over her head, just the way she used to do when she was a little kid and got scared of something. She'd even considered finding her old teddy bear and taking it to bed with her for comfort.

Did Marybeth ever get scared and take any of her teddy bears to bed? She probably would if she saw a mummy.

The bright morning sunlight reassured Bonnie that the mummy had been just a figment of her imagination. Or maybe a trick of the moonlight. Sometimes things looked like something they weren't when the moon was bright.

Still, just to make sure, she went out to the backyard before she left for school and searched the spot where she'd seen the mummy standing. There wouldn't be any footprints. The grass was too thick. So what was she expecting to see? Maybe a jewel that had dropped from its dark eye sockets? *Get real, Bonnie,* she told herself. There hadn't been any mummy out there.

But when she turned to go back to the house, she saw a scrap of white cloth caught on a branch of a thorny pyracantha bush. Almost reluctantly she walked over to it. She didn't really want to see anything that would prove there *had* been a mummy standing in the darkness of her backyard.

But the scrap of cloth was there, not white but yellowed. And brittle. As if it had been around for a long, long time.

Her heart thudding, Bonnie turned and ran for the house. She left the scrap of ancient cloth where it was. She didn't really want to touch it.

There had to be a perfectly innocent explanation. Even if Nazli had located a mummy, it wouldn't be here already, would it? And certainly it wouldn't be walking around. So if Bonnie *had* seen something out there in the moonlight, it would have been someone playing a trick on her. But who would do that?

And why had the figure beckoned to her? What did it want her to do?

She didn't say anything to her family. She could just imagine how Halden would hoot if she said she'd seen a mummy in the backyard.

Nazli came to school that day in golden sandals and a straight, ivory-colored, sleeveless dress that hung almost to her ankles. A glittery gold belt was draped loosely over her hips, and she wore a snake around her head like a sweatband. It wasn't really a snake, of course. It was made of metal and had a snake head in front that raised up about two inches.

She looked very Egyptian.

She was standing at the bottom of the stairs leading to the school when Bonnie got there. Kids looked at her as they passed, and some of them snickered and poked their friends.

Bonnie hesitated at the top of the stairs. Nazli was waiting for her. But did she really want to join her?

Then she was ashamed of herself. She knew well enough what it was like to be made fun of. It hurt.

"Nazli," she called as she hurried down the stairs. "You look cute!"

Somebody snorted, but Bonnie didn't turn to see who it was.

It was loud enough so that certainly Nazli heard it too, but she didn't react. Instead she grinned at Bonnie and tossed back her long, black hair. "Just call me Cleopatra," she said. "I wore this today to show you how you might want to dress for the Egyptian room at your spook alley." Clasping her hands in front of herself, she shifted her head back and forth in a snaky movement Bonnie had seen dancers on TV do.

Bonnie knew that kids were staring, but she said, "It's terrific, Nazli. We'll have the best room at the party."

"Especially when I get the mummy," Nazli said.

The bell rang, calling everybody to class.

"Nazli," Bonnie said as they hurried toward their classroom, "speaking of mummies, did you dress up like one last night and come to my house?"

Nazli looked at her blankly. "Of course not. Why?"

"Forget it," Bonnie said. There wasn't time to explain.

She didn't bring the subject up again. But all day long she looked around the classroom, wondering who might have heard what she and Nazli had said yesterday and gotten inspired to appear at her house as a mummy. A mummy wrapped in ancient, yellowed winding cloths.

Nobody looked guilty except Trent MacAfee, whose ears got red when he saw her looking at him.

Nobody was home when Bonnie got there after school. She went to her room to change into some old cut-off jeans and her comforting, furry, bear-claw slippers, then went to the refrigerator to get a drink of orange juice.

Sport was asleep with his head against the door, so she had to push him out of the way first. As she did, she saw a note from her mom taped to the refrigerator door, the family communications center. "Call Sister Jackson," her mom had written, "about doing a service project. She says she has one that's perfect for you."

After Bonnie had her drink of orange juice, she went to the phone and punched in Sister Jackson's number. She was curious about who would be "perfect" for her to serve. Somebody with enormous feet and stringy hair? Someone who hung around with people who thought they had once been Cleopatra?

Sister Jackson answered after the first ring. "Bonnie," she said, "I think you know how we assign each girl in the Young Women to do a service project for somebody in the ward who needs help."

"Yes," Bonnie said. "I know about that."

"I have a project for you," Sister Jackson said. "I've

checked it out with your mother. She thinks you'll enjoy doing it."

Bonnie wasn't sure what to say about that. Mothers could be tricky. Sometimes their ideas about what kids would enjoy were not very cool.

"Oh," she said.

"Do you know Sister Wyndam in our ward?" Sister Jackson went on.

Who didn't? Kids called her "The Witch of Whipple Street." Sister Wyndam lived alone in a big house surrounded by trees. She didn't come to church very often, but when she did she sat alone in the back of the chapel and rushed out right after sacrament meeting, before anyone could speak to her.

Every Halloween Sister Wyndam decorated her house and yard like some people decorated for Christmas, only she used Halloween stuff—tombstones and skeletons and witches on broomsticks. She strung ghost lights on the bushes, and always had a huge, toothy, orange jack-o-lantern face frowning down from her roof. Lots of people took their kids to see the house, but Sister Wyndam never came outside to greet them.

"I know her," Bonnie said.

"She could use some help right now," Sister Jackson said.

Well, why not? Bonnie looked into the little mirror that hung over the phone table. She twisted a lock of her limp hair. Maybe she should call Nazli and have her go along too. Maybe the three of them could form a group called "Weirdos Anonymous." They ought to get along fine together.

"Okay," Bonnie said. "I'll help her."

"Actually," Sister Jackson said, "you'll be working with her grandson."

Grandson. Bonnie thought of some lumpy Scout who would spot her big feet right away and start a campaign to make her miserable. Forget it.

Her hand tightened on the phone. How was she going to get out of this? "Well . . ." she started.

"He's nine," Sister Jackson continued. "He's confined to a wheelchair and can't attend school at the moment. He'll be living with Sister Wyndam for a while."

Nine. A kid. Bonnie liked kids.

"Why's he in a wheelchair?" she asked. "What will I be doing? I don't know anything about being a nurse."

"I don't know the full story," Sister Jackson said. "But what you'll be doing is helping him keep up with his schoolwork and probably playing computer games with him. He's a smart boy."

"I'd like that," Bonnie said.

"Good." Bonnie could hear Sister Jackson shuffling some papers, probably checking off one more thing done. "I'll call Sister Wyndam and have her get in touch with you."

After a few more words, they hung up.

Bonnie felt good about accepting the project. It would make her feel more like one of the Beehives, who, she knew, all had service projects. As far as she knew, the other girls all were assigned to older people. That would have been okay, but she was glad she'd been assigned to a kid.

Besides, she might be able to pick up some really great Halloween ideas from Sister Wyndam.

Thinking of Halloween reminded her again of the mummy she thought she had seen in the backyard last night, and of the scrap of old, yellowed cloth she'd found that morning, caught on the pyracantha bush.

Was it still there, or had that been her imagination too?

Nervously she went to the back door and peered out. She couldn't see the bush clearly.

She opened the door, then hesitated, scuffing her bear-claw slippers against the floor. She called Sport to come with her, but he gave an enormous yawn and flopped down again with his head against the refrigerator door.

Forget him. She didn't need an escort. Or did she? Maybe she should wait until somebody else came home. Maybe she should show the scrap to the rest of her family. At least to her dad. He wouldn't make fun of her like Halden would. Dad was a chemistry teacher. Maybe he could even test the scrap of cloth to see if it actually was as ancient as it looked.

First she'd better make sure it was still there, before she told her family anything.

Taking a deep breath, she walked out the door and across the lawn. Already she could see that the scrap of cloth *was* still there.

She approached it cautiously, then laughed at herself for being such a wimp. Was the cloth going to bite her? Even if it should be a piece of a mummy's winding cloth, it wasn't going to do anything except hang there on the twig that had caught it.

This time she walked right up to the bush and bent down to examine the cloth. She still didn't want to touch it. Besides, in all the mystery shows she'd seen on TV, the authorities always said you should never tamper with evidence.

Was this evidence? Evidence of what? That a mummy had been there?

There wasn't a whole lot to see. The scrap was about six inches long and maybe three inches wide.

It was yellowish and looked brittle, just as she'd seen that morning.

What she hadn't seen that morning was something sort of bluish-gray on one end of the scrap. What was that? Mold, maybe? Mold from a mummy?

Bonnie stepped quickly backward and was startled when she bumped against someone who must have crept up behind her.

Her heart slammed against her ribs as a voice said, "Bonnie, I've come to take you away."

CHAPTER
7

Bonnie thought her heart would leap out of her chest. She heard it thudding as she whirled around to see who had spoken. If a mummy was standing there, it would be hello, heaven, because she would die on the spot.

But it wasn't a mummy. It was Sister Jackson, her Beehive teacher.

"Oh, I'm sorry," Sister Jackson said. "I didn't mean to frighten you like that. I thought you heard me coming. I saw you come back here, so I just followed instead of ringing the doorbell." She put a hand on Bonnie's arm as if to prop her up. "Are you okay?"

Bonnie sagged against her. "I think so," she quavered, then straightened up. "I wasn't expecting anybody to be here." She should have brought Sport outside with her after all. He always barked at strangers and would have given her warning.

"I'm sorry," Sister Jackson said again. "I guess you were thinking about something else."

She had *that* right. Bonnie had been thinking about the mummy that had left the scrap of cloth on the bush. Should she show it to Sister Jackson?

No. It was too weird. She didn't want to say anything to *anybody* until she could figure out what was going on and be sure she wasn't imagining things. Or at least until she could talk to Nazli about it.

"Yes," she said. "I *was* thinking about something else." She didn't have to say any more than that.

"Again, I'm sorry I frightened you." Sister Jackson took her hand away from Bonnie's arm now that she was steady. "But I've come to take you away to another time."

Another time? "Huh?" Bonnie said.

"It's a kidnap supper," Sister Jackson explained. "We don't do this every year because we like it to be a surprise when nobody's expecting it. The Young Women officers and teachers whisk the girls away for an evening of food and fun. Come along, now. We're going to Sister LeFevre's house. I called your mother earlier, so she knows all about it."

"Oh," Bonnie said. "Oh." She took a deep breath.

Her heart had slowed down almost to normal. "Was that why she left the note telling me to call you?"

"Partially," Sister Jackson admitted. "I wanted to make sure you were home. But I also wanted to tell you about your service project assignment. I think you're going to enjoy working with Sister Wyndam's grandson."

"I think so too." Bonnie started toward the house. "Come in while I change."

"Uh-uh-uh," Sister Jackson said. "It's a come-as-you-are event. That's part of the fun."

"Like this?" Bonnie looked down at her tattered, cut-off jeans and her embarrassingly huge bear-claw slippers.

Sister Jackson laughed. "You should see some of the other girls. Let's go." She walked toward the street, motioning for Bonnie to follow her.

Bonnie hesitated. What were the perfect Bee Theres going to say when they saw her? They'd never let her into their club when they saw how she slopped around at home.

And what about that scrap of cloth? Should she just leave it hanging there on the bush?

She didn't have much choice. Sister Jackson turned around, walked back, and took her hand. "Come on, Bonnie. You'll enjoy this party. Trust me."

Bonnie went.

Becca, her sister Loni, and Sunshine were already in the backseat of Sister Jackson's car. They laughed when they saw Bonnie, but it wasn't you're-really-a-freak laughter. It was the kind that said, "Hey, don't we all look gross!" They piled out of the car and pranced around, giving Bonnie a fashion show.

Becca wore one of her dad's old shirts with the sleeves cut off. It hung down past her knees, and there were paint splatters all over it. Her feet were bare.

Bonnie couldn't even begin to guess what it was that Sunshine was wearing. The skirt hung in different lengths and the top had long, full sleeves that looked as if they'd been shredded. She wore a pair of thick-soled, lace-up boots on her feet.

Actually, her outfit wasn't so different from her school clothes, which always looked as if she'd gotten them from a ragbag. The thing was, they looked good on Sunshine, as if they should be the latest fashion.

Loni's hair was rolled up in hot curlers, and she had paste-on eyelashes attached to one eyelid.

She grinned when she saw Bonnie looking at her. "I was figuring out what I want to do for the homecoming dance," she explained.

Loni was sixteen and was a friend of Bonnie's sister, Priscilla. She had a date for the homecoming dance.

Bonnie couldn't imagine liking a guy well enough to want to spend a whole evening with him. All the guys her age were dopey and they teased her. Besides, they were all shorter than she was.

Loni looked back at the house as they all got into Sister Jackson's car. "Where's Priscilla?" she asked. "How comes she's escaping this adventure?"

Bonnie wondered that too. Priscilla hadn't come home from school yet.

Sister Jackson smiled. "She isn't escaping. Her mother said she was staying at school to practice for a water ballet. Somebody's going to pick her up at the pool."

"In her *swimsuit?*" Bonnie asked.

Sister Jackson nodded. "Probably. As I said, it's a come-as-you-are party."

Prissy Priscilla was going to hate that. She'd probably refuse to come.

Sister LeFevre's house was on Whipple Street, right next to Sister Wyndam's. As Sister Jackson stopped the car, Bonnie peered at the house next door, hoping to catch a glimpse of the little boy who would be her service project. She still had all her old Dr. Seuss books. Would he want her to read them to him? Would he like ghost stories? Could she tell him about the mummy?

Bonnie pictured him, pale and thin, reclining in

his wheelchair with a faint smile on his little face as she read to him. He would beg her to stay longer and read more, and she'd share all the books she loved with him.

Thinking about it almost made her eyes mist up.

But there was nobody to be seen at Sister Wyndam's big house. All of its windows were shuttered, as if it had its eyes closed. It didn't look like a very cheerful place for a sick little boy in a wheelchair.

There were several girls standing on the steps of Sister LeFevre's house. One of them was Priscilla. And yes, she *was* wearing her swimsuit, although she had a skimpy towel wrapped around herself. Both her suit and her hair were still wet, which was okay for a hot October day in southern California.

The girls on the steps waited for those in Sister Jackson's car to catch up before they all went in.

"Isn't this fun?" Priscilla said to Bonnie as they walked together into Sister LeFevre's spacious living room. "Didn't I tell you that you'd love Beehives?"

It surprised Bonnie that Priscilla was being such a good sport about coming in her swimsuit. If she could be happy that way, certainly Bonnie could make it with her big bear-claw slippers.

For the first time Bonnie believed it might be true that she would love being a Beehive girl.

The other members of the Beehive class were already there. Carlie was in her pajamas. "I'd just thrown all my school clothes into the washing machine when I got kidnapped," she said. Marybeth was dressed in a bathrobe and wore a towel around her head, as if she'd just gotten out of a shower. Elena was okay in black shorts and a bright red blouse, and Ducky wore blue jeans with a T-shirt that said, "School is cool."

"My dad gave it to me," she explained every time somebody groaned about the message. "I only wear it around home."

Ducky's dad was the principal of the junior high that all the Beehives except Bonnie attended.

Bonnie was surprised when everybody liked her enormous bear-claw slippers.

"They're neat," one girl said. "I love the claws."

"I'm a stand-in for Bigfoot on his day off," Bonnie said.

To her amazement, the girls laughed.

They're nice, she thought. Why had she ever been afraid of them?

"She rents them out on cold nights," Priscilla said, and the girls laughed again.

Bonnie held up one of her feet so they could see better. "They each sleep six," she said.

This time the other Beehives cheered, and Marybeth said, "That's our Bonnie."

Bonnie felt as if she must be glowing. Now surely they would ask her to join the Bee Theres. It wasn't so hard to fit in after all, once a person relaxed a little.

Before she could say anything else, Sister LeFevre clapped her hands for attention.

"I guess you've noticed all the antiques around the room," she said.

To tell the truth, Bonnie had been so taken up with the popularity of her slippers that she hadn't noticed. But now she remembered that Sister Jackson had said she was taking her away "to another time."

"We've taken you back to pioneer times," Sister LeFevre said when all the girls were quiet. She motioned toward the antiques. "These are the things your great-grandmother used in her daily life. Who would like to try out her washing machine?" She pointed at an old galvanized washtub sitting on a bench. Inside it was propped a well-used scrubbing board.

One of the older girls volunteered. She picked up a soggy piece of clothing from the tub and rubbed it up and down on the scrubbing board. "It's hard on the knuckles," she commented.

"How about great-grandmother's iron?" Sister

LeFevre asked. "You don't plug this one in. There's a handle with three irons that it hooks onto. You iron with the first one until it gets cold, then go to your old black cookstove—heated by putting wood in the firebox—and get a hot one. Then you iron again. Who wants to demonstrate?"

She held the iron out toward Bonnie.

Bonnie took it and went to the old wooden ironing board standing next to the piano. There was a cloth spread on the ironing board, a yellowed cloth that looked old and brittle. One of its edges was rough, as if a strip had been torn from it.

The cloth looked just like the scrap that was caught on the bush in her backyard.

It was all she could do not to drop the iron and back away from that yellowed square of cloth.

But how would she explain what had startled her? If she started whimpering about mummy-winding cloths, the girls would think she had totally weirded out and she'd be right back to square one.

She managed to run the heavy iron back and forth across the cloth a few times, then hefted it in the air. "Good for aerobics, too," she said.

The girls laughed.

She had handled that okay, but she barely saw the next demonstration, which was churning butter. She was thinking too much about that piece of old cloth. Who had brought it?

Maybe she could watch who took it home at the end of the evening. Maybe that would give her a clue as to who was appearing in her backyard as a mummy.

After the demonstrations, Sister LeFevre said, "We can't resist the temptation to teach a lesson even at a party."

All the girls groaned.

Sister LeFevre smiled and went on. "A lot of our pioneer ancestors had to leave their homes just as abruptly as you did today. Especially those who were driven out of Nauvoo. They had to grab what they could and start the trek that took them to the Salt Lake Valley."

The girls were quiet as they thought of the oft-repeated story.

What Bonnie thought of was the square of cloth that looked old enough to have come with the pioneers. Older, even. Old enough to have come from a mummy. Couldn't she just ask Sister LeFevre where it had come from?

Sister LeFevre was still speaking. "Nowadays we have to be prepared for disasters, like the 1993 earthquake and fires, that could drive us out of our homes. What would you do it you had to leave your home just as you are right now? What if you had to survive without running water, without heat, without electricity?"

"What, no hair dryers?" somebody said.

"I mean not anything except what you have with you right now," Sister LeFevre said. "So while we finish preparing our pioneer supper of beans and cornbread, I want all of you to go out to my backyard and figure out one thing that would help you survive, if you no longer had access to your house. We'll discuss it after we eat."

Bonnie started to follow the chattering girls outside, but then turned back and approached Sister LeFevre.

"Uh," she said, not sure how she should explain this. "Uh," she repeated. "Uh, I just wondered where that piece of old cloth came from."

"What cloth?" Sister LeFevre looked around.

"The one that I ironed. It seemed really old."

Sister LeFevre looked a little puzzled. "I guess it is."

"Uh," Bonnie said, "where did you get it?"

Looking even more puzzled, Sister LeFevre said, "I'm not sure who gave it to me. I was getting antiques and old things from everybody. I asked all the moms I talked to if they had something that looked as if it came from pioneer times. Almost everybody has an old, yellowed sheet or two hanging around." She peered at Bonnie. "Do you want it? Have you got some idea of how to use it in a survival situation?"

"No," Bonnie said, "although I guess you could use it for bandages if you didn't have anything else." Maybe that would take away Sister LeFevre's puzzled look. "Well," she went on, "I guess I'll go look for something else to survive with."

She went outside, embarrassed that she'd said anything. It had made Sister LeFevre think she was strange, and she certainly hadn't learned anything. The cloth could have come from anywhere.

Certainly there had to be more than one piece of old, yellowed cloth in the world. Why couldn't she just forget it?

It was a hard thing to forget.

But why worry about it? The mummy, or the person dressed like a mummy, hadn't tried to hurt her in any way, had it?

"We could cut down the trees," somebody said in her ear.

It was Marybeth. "For fuel," she said when Bonnie looked at her blankly. "To survive," she explained further when Bonnie didn't say anything.

"Oh," Bonnie said. "Sure. If you happened to grab an axe on your way out of your house."

Marybeth chuckled.

Bonnie looked around, wondering what she could suggest as a survival aid. Walking over to the tall eucalyptus trees that marked the property lines between Sister LeFevre's place and Sister Wyndam's, she put a hand on one of the shaggy trunks. She could see Sister Wyndam's neat brick patio from there. She hadn't been able to see that from the street.

On the patio was a wheelchair, turned so Bonnie couldn't see who was in it. It had to be Sister Wyndam's grandson, Bonnie's service project, the pale little nine-year-old boy to whom she'd be reading stories.

This was a good chance to get acquainted. She might even talk to Sister Wyndam right now and pick up some ideas for the Halloween party.

Bonnie stepped forward. Suddenly she sprawled on the ground, her feet snared in a loop of rope that pulled tight and raised her legs several inches off the ground.

As she struggled to get up, she saw the wheelchair whirl around. A red-haired, freckle-faced kid, built like a miniature football player, peered at her.

"Well," the kid said. "It looks like I just caught Bigfoot."

CHAPTER
8

Bonnie lay there looking silently up at the boy who gazed at her from his wheelchair. This was just a temporary setback, she told herself. Things had been so good for a little while; they'd be good again soon.

"Did you set this trap?" she asked calmly.

The boy nodded. "Serves you right," he said. "What were you doing snooping around here?"

"I wasn't snooping." Bonnie struggled to get loose. The rope tightened around her legs and raised them higher. "I was . . ." She stopped. Maybe she shouldn't tell him she was coming over to get acquainted because he was going to be her service project. Maybe she should just tell Sister Jackson that she couldn't do it. This kid just wouldn't do.

She struggled to sit up as far as she could and began yanking at the rope.

"Won't do any good," the kid said. "The more you yank, the tighter it'll get."

That sounded like some of the things Mom said. "The hurrieder you go, the behinder you get." "The more you try to impress somebody, the more likely you are to fall on your face."

"Okay," Bonnie said. "You tell me how to get out of this, then."

The kid wheeled his chair closer. "Why should I?" He narrowed his eyes. "I should call my grandma. I should call the police. You were trespassing."

Bonnie wished she could reach the kid. She'd . . . she'd what? You didn't whack people in wheelchairs.

She struggled again with the rope.

"Look," she said, "I admit I shouldn't have wandered over onto your grandma's property. But I didn't mean any harm. I'm just at a party over there." She pointed at Sister LeFevre's house.

"I know," the kid said. "I heard you all laughing. People are always laughing in that house."

"Maybe you should go over there someday and learn how." The words were out before Bonnie could stop them.

The kid looked at her for a long moment. Then he said, "First, don't panic. Relax. Don't fight the rope. Look the situation over. What's your brain for?

Don't you ever play computer games that make you think things through?"

Nasty little kid, sitting there enjoying the whole thing. Bonnie had thought she'd be getting a *nice* little boy as a service project, not a smarty-party, computer-wise brat who trapped her, then obviously enjoyed watching her struggle.

She glared at him, but that didn't get her out of the problem.

Don't fight the rope. Look the situation over.

Okay, so she looked it over. She was lying half-buried in a pile of dead leaves, her big bear-claw feet securely bound together by the rope.

One thing she could do was yell for help.

But then everybody would see what a klutz, what a dumdum, what a loser she was. She'd be right back to being poor old Bonnie with the big, clumsy feet.

Or she could do what the kid advised and think herself out of this.

She pulled. The rope tightened. The kid was right.

She relaxed. The rope loosened. She hitched forward, lifting her legs a little, giving the rope more slack.

Reaching up, she flipped off the bear-claw slippers, then slid her feet out of the rope.

She was free.

She stood up, putting her feet back in the slippers.

"Now listen here," she began, advancing toward the kid.

Suddenly he grinned. "My name's Milford," he said. "Don't you hate it? What's *your* name?"

Bonnie paused, feeling off balance. Her mouth was open, still ready to lay a bunch of really heavy words on the obnoxious kid.

On Milford.

It *was* a pretty bad name.

And he looked like an entirely different boy when he grinned.

She closed her mouth. "I'm Bonnie."

She wanted to demand that he tell her why he'd set the trap. She wanted to know why he had to stay with his grandmother, Sister Wyndam. She wanted to ask what had happened to put him in a wheelchair.

But he *was* in a wheelchair. She'd better not demand anything.

"I have to go," she said, running off before Milford could say more.

She met Sunshine, Marybeth, and Elena just around the corner of the house.

"Bonnie," Sunshine said as if she were glad to see her. "We were getting worried about you."

Elena came up and gave Bonnie a hug, saying, "Where did you disappear to?"

Bonnie felt good in spite of the rocky meeting with Milford. The other girls had missed her.

"I was getting a lesson in survival skills," Bonnie said, which was pretty much the truth.

Later, when it was her turn to offer something to the other girls that would help them to survive in a disaster, she said, "Don't panic."

"That's good, Bonnie," Sister LeFevre said. "That's one of the first things we should all remember."

Don't panic, Bonnie told herself. *Don't panic about what to do for the Phantom Fair. Don't panic if the mummy shows up again. Good advice.*

So why did she panic later that night when the mummy appeared again under the trees in her backyard?

She shivered as she stood at her window looking out at the bright, moonlit night. She could see the mummy quite clearly now, its unraveling winding cloths, its arms, one of which hung down by its side while the other seemed bound to its chest.

As she watched, it beckoned to her. Then it shuffled slowly forward, inch by inch, dragging one foot, like the mummy in the old movies *The Mummy's Ghost* or *The Mummy's Hand* that her family used to watch sometimes after family home evening.

Should she yell for her family now? From downstairs she heard the sound of hollow, tinny laughter. She knew that her mom and dad were down there watching their favorite show and that the laughter came from the TV, but suddenly it seemed as if the mummy was mocking her.

She tried to take a look at the total situation, the way that kid Milford had said. First she replayed the thoughts she'd had when she'd seen the yellowed cloth on the ironing board at Sister LeFevre's house. Anybody could have old cloth lying around. Just because there was a scrap of ancient-looking material out there on the bush in her backyard, it didn't mean a real, live mummy was wandering around.

Suddenly Bonnie laughed at herself. What did she mean, "real, live mummy"? There were real, live *people,* but mummies were dead, dead, dead. They didn't wander around.

Except in Nazli's strange world.

Don't panic. Think the situation through.

Okay, what she needed to do was talk to Nazli.

In fact, she was going to tell Nazli to forget the mummy. She would plan something else for the Beehives' contribution to the Phantom Fair.

But what?

Glancing at her bedside clock, she saw that it was too late to call Nazli that night. So she'd talk to her at school.

When she looked out the window again, the mummy was gone.

The next morning everybody except Dad was in the kitchen when Bonnie came downstairs ready for school. Halden was shoveling cornflakes into his mouth, and Priscilla was nibbling a piece of toast.

"Dad has already gone to work and will be late getting home tonight," Mom said. "And Halden and I are going to spend the afternoon in the garment district in downtown L.A. There aren't too many days left before he leaves for the Missionary Training Center in Provo, and we haven't got all the clothes he'll need."

Bonnie remembered the long list Halden had gotten from Salt Lake City telling him what he should take with him to Romania. No wonder he and Mom were going to the garment district, where they were likelier to find bargain prices.

"So," Mom continued, "do you girls think you can make dinner for yourselves?" Mom looked at Priscilla and Bonnie. "Halden and I can't go until he puts in a half day at work, which means we might as well eat dinner downtown as to sit somewhere in rush-hour traffic. Dad will grab a bite near his office."

Priscilla looked at Bonnie. "How about it, Bon? Can we do it?"

Her attitude toward Bonnie had seemed to change since the kidnap supper last night, almost as if she now saw her as a friend rather than a little sister. Of course, she didn't know about how Bonnie had gotten hung up in Milford's trap and the way he said he'd caught Bigfoot and how he'd had to tell her how to get out of the rope. Bonnie hadn't told anybody about that.

"Sure we can handle it," Bonnie said. "Don't panic."

They giggled together.

"That's an in joke," Priscilla explained to Mom. "Did you know our Bon and those ratty slippers of hers were a real hit last night?"

Halden looked up from his cereal and raised his eyebrows. "Those grossious, atrocious bear-claw disasters?"

Even Halden's teasing seemed good-natured this morning. Bonnie grinned happily. Maybe she was joining the human race after all.

"Send me a picture of those feet while I'm on my mission," Halden said. "My companions will never believe it!"

"I'll send two pictures," Bonnie said, "since I can't get both feet into one picture."

Halden laughed.

Mom seemed pleased that her children, who were generally bickering about something or other, were actually having fun together. "Why don't you each have a girlfriend over for dinner?" she said to Priscilla and Bonnie.

"I'll invite Nazli," Bonnie said. She could tell Nazli about how she'd been trapped by that kid Milford. Nazli would understand.

And she could tell Nazli then to cancel the mummy.

Halden's eyebrows went up further. "Nazli? Cleopatra, you mean? Wish I could be here."

Halden loved to argue with Nazli about reincarnation versus resurrection and a lot of other stuff Bonnie wasn't sure she understood, although Nazli seemed to know about it.

Nazli would know what to do about the scrap of cloth caught on the bush in the backyard.

That day at school, Nazli said she'd be delighted to come to dinner and declared that she'd like to help fix it. She called her mother at noon for permission; it was all right with her, as long as Nazli was home by 7:00 to do her chores and homework. Then

Nazli and Bonnie talked about what they'd like to cook. Nazli said she wished they could make *shwarma,* which was something Middle Eastern, but she said you usually fixed that only for a crowd. "Or maybe we could do something Greek, like *dolmades,*" she said. "Do you happen to have grape leaves on hand?"

Bonnie shook her head.

"Okay, then," Nazli said, "how about *mousaka?* How about *pollo alla cacciatore?*"

"How about hot dogs?" Bonnie said.

"Perfect," Nazli agreed.

"Do you eat that kind of stuff all the time at your house?" Bonnie asked. "*Shwarma,* I mean, and *Moose-whatever-it-is.*"

Nazli laughed, her teeth flashing white against the background of her olive skin. "Gosh, no. My mom cooks chicken or hamburgers most of the time, just like everybody else."

Sometimes Nazli bewildered Bonnie, and this was one of those times. "Why were you suggesting all that fancy stuff, then?"

Nazli shrugged. "For effect, I guess. I do things for effect, Bonnie."

Bonnie wasn't exactly sure what she meant, but she let it go. Nazli wasn't wearing her Cleopatra clothes that day. In fact, she looked like just any ordinary girl, in blue jeans and a deep red T-shirt. Bonnie was always happier to be seen with her when she wore normal clothes.

Nobody teased either one of them that day. Bonnie couldn't help but feel that her life had suddenly started off in a new direction. She liked it.

Priscilla didn't bring home a friend for dinner. She said she had to finish her homework before Mutual that night. Hot dogs were fine with her. She put together a salad while Nazli and Bonnie grilled the franks and warmed the buns they found in the freezer.

After they ate, they all cleaned up the kitchen; then Priscilla went upstairs to study.

"Let's watch TV for a while before you have to go," Bonnie said. She was feeling really good because everything had been going so well, and she wondered if she should even bring up the subject of the mummy.

On the other hand, this was probably the exact right time to talk about it, when things were going so well.

"Nazli," she said after they were seated in the family room, "have you contacted a mummy yet?"

Nazli switched TV channels with the remote control. "No, but I'm working on it."

"Well," Bonnie said, "the night after we talked,

there was a mummy in my backyard. I mean, probably it was a person dressed like a mummy."

Nazli's head turned quickly toward Bonnie. Her eyes darkened. "Where exactly was it?" Her voice was tight.

Bonnie pointed out the kitchen window. "Out there. Under the trees."

Nazli sprang to her feet. "Show me." She headed for the door. "Did it leave anything?"

Bonnie felt as if her throat had closed. "Yes," she said. "A strip of old, yellowy cloth."

Nazli put a hand to her mouth. "Oh, no," she whispered. She stopped and stared silently out at the trees.

"Nazli," Bonnie said. "What's the matter?"

Nazli looked back at her, and her eyes seemed as big as her face. "It's Nesmut," she said.

"It's what?" Bonnie asked, bewildered.

"Not *what. Who,*" Nazli said. "Nesmut was one of my handmaidens. She always hated me. She was jealous. I was the queen Cleopatra, and she was a slave." She turned to look at Bonnie. "Are you sure about the cloth?"

Bonnie felt as if her throat had closed up. "Yes," she squeaked. "It got caught on a bush."

Nazli nodded. "Nesmut always leaves a scrap of her winding linen," she said, "as a warning." She clutched Bonnie's arm. "You didn't touch it, did you?"

"No."

Nazli was shaking her head. "I'm sorry. I don't always have control over which of the ancients answers my call." She looked out at the trees, which seemed dark and menacing in the late-afternoon light. "Nesmut is bad news, Bonnie."

Great, Bonnie thought. It was just her luck to have a troublemaking mummy show up right when she'd had a taste of things going fairly well for a change.

CHAPTER
9

Nazli continued to stand there, looking out at the trees.

"Don't you want to see the piece of cloth?" Bonnie asked. "Maybe you can tell if it's real winding linen or not. Maybe somebody's just playing a trick on me."

"*Nesmut* is playing a trick on you, Bonnie," Nazli said. "She'll foul up everything you try to do."

Bonnie figured she didn't need Nesmut to do that. She was pretty good at fouling up everything all on her own.

"Well," Bonnie said, "tell her to go back where she came from. I've decided I don't want a mummy for our Phantom Fair after all. Cancel her."

Nazli shook her head again. "You can't just delete a mummy after you've called it up, like you'd get rid of a word on your computer. Nesmut is bad news, Bonnie. She'll be here until she's caused enough mischief to satisfy herself for another hundred years."

This sounded like big-time serious stuff. Bonnie cleared her throat. "Well, just how bad is she?"

"She used to put snakes in my bed," Nazli said. "You know how history books say Cleopatra died from a snake bite?"

Bonnie remembered reading that.

"Who do you think brought the snake?" Nazli said. "You remember how the books say I purposely let a snake bite me because I wanted to die?"

Bonnie was caught up in the story. "That wasn't true?"

Nazli rolled her eyes. "What do *you* think?"

Bonnie tried to imagine the beautiful Queen of the Nile actually inviting a snake to bite her. No, it must have been Nesmut's doing.

But what about the history books? Would they have stuff in them that wasn't true?

On the other hand, if Nazli had actually been Cleopatra, she should know whether she had killed herself on purpose or not, shouldn't she?

Could Nazli have been Cleopatra?

"Let's go get that piece of cloth," Bonnie said. "Maybe I should give it back to Nesmut next time she comes."

91

Nazli followed her out the door. "Maybe you should."

This time Bonnie made Sport come out to the backyard. He hadn't barked at Nazli because she'd been at Bonnie's house before, but Bonnie wanted him with her in case somebody sneaked up on her again, as Sister Jackson had done.

"Maybe I should grab the mummy next time I see her," Bonnie said, "just to make sure she's *really* a mummy."

Bonnie thought Nazli might object to that, but she didn't. She nodded solemnly. "That would be one way to find out. Look, let's go scope out that scrap of linen and I'll see if I can get more clues."

Bonnie led the way across the lawn to the trees where she'd seen the mummy. "It's right over here on this bush." She pointed toward the bush that had snagged the piece of cloth.

But there was nothing on it except what belonged on a bush.

Branches and twigs and leaves. No scrap of ancient, yellowed linen.

Nazli looked the bush over. "I don't see it."

"That's because it's not here." Bonnie went over to touch the twig where the scrap of cloth had hung, as if that would make it reappear. Sport came over to sniff the bush.

"The wind probably blew it away," Bonnie said.

"Probably Nesmut came and got it." Nazli's eyes darkened. "Maybe she's already up to something."

Was Nazli right? Was Nesmut already causing trouble?

Sport began barking and ran around the side of the house.

"Someone's coming," Bonnie said. "He always barks at strangers."

From the front of the house somebody called, "Bonnie?"

It sounded like Carlie. What would Carlie be doing at her house?

"We'll talk about this later," Bonnie told Nazli. "Come with me." She headed for a path that led around the side of the house, motioning for Nazli to follow. The path was a little muddy, evidence that Mom or Halden or somebody had been doing some watering in the backyard in the past couple of days.

That wasn't unusual. But what was unusual were the footprints in the soft mud. They didn't look as if they'd been made by shoes, although they were foot shaped. They hadn't been made by bare feet, either.

Mummy feet, maybe? Feet wrapped in layers of linen?

"Nazli," Bonnie called, "come look at these."

There was silence behind her.

"Nazli?" Bonnie turned to look for her friend, but there was no one there.

What had happened to Nazli? She hadn't said she was leaving. She hadn't said anything at all.

"Bonnie?" someone called again; then Carlie, followed by Marybeth, Sunshine, Becca, Elena, and Ducky, came around the corner of the house.

Sport barked louder than ever.

"Quiet!" Bonnie yelled at him.

Offended, he drooped his head and slunk around to the back of the house.

"Hi," Sunshine said. "We didn't mean to scare your dog."

"That's okay." Bonnie looked in the direction Sport had gone. "He'll probably go back in the house. He sleeps by the refrigerator all day hoping that somebody will give him a snack."

"Sounds like my dog," Sunshine said. "Her name's Brunhilda." She peered behind Bonnie. "Who were you talking to a minute ago?"

"Nazli." Bonnie was bewildered. "She was here. I don't know where she went. Did she come out ahead of me?"

The girls looked at one another. "We didn't see her," Ducky said.

"But she couldn't have gone out any other way." Bonnie looked behind her at the empty yard.

94

"There's a wall back there. It's too high to jump over. And she couldn't just disappear, like the cloth. Could she?"

The girls gazed at the backyard, then at one another again.

What were they thinking? That she was crazy? Why couldn't things be like last night, when they'd all thought she was cute and funny and like everybody else?

Bonnie kept her eyes from looking again at the footprints in the mud. There was no way she was going to mention them right now. Or the mummy.

She tried a friendly smile. "So," she said to the girls, "what's up?"

"Uh," Marybeth said, peering behind her, "don't you think we should go look for Nazli?"

"No," Bonnie said. "She's probably all right."

"Probably?" Marybeth's voice went up at the end of the word.

"Oh—maybe we *should* go look for her," Bonnie said quickly, wishing she could play this whole scene over again.

"We'll help you," Elena said, walking right across the muddy footprints without looking down.

The girls fanned out across the yard, searching behind trees and under bushes. Bonnie went to the back wall. It was high, but Nazli was athletic. Perhaps she could have gone over it.

If she hadn't, then the only explanation was that Nesmut had snatched her away, like she'd taken the piece of cloth.

"We didn't find anything," Marybeth said as the girls came back to join Bonnie, "except this." She held up a strip of old, yellowed cloth.

"What was Nazli wearing?" Becca asked. "Could that be a piece of her clothes?"

Bonnie took the scrap of material. It looked like the same one that had been on the bush earlier. *What was going on?* Was it the Bee Theres who were doing all this mummy business? But why would they do that to her? To torment her? To scare her out of the Beehive class?

"Where did you find this?" she asked, trying to keep her voice normal.

"Back on that bush." Marybeth pointed at the same bush that Bonnie had examined earlier—the one that had sported only branches, twigs, and leaves.

Don't panic, Bonnie told herself. Think. If they had put the cloth there in the first place, they would know where it had been and would naturally say that was where they had gotten it.

But she couldn't believe the Bee Theres would play tricks like that on her. Would they?

Oh, what was the matter with her? She was suspecting everybody now. She must be totally losing it.

Bonnie crumpled the cloth and shoved it into her jeans pocket. "This isn't from Nazli's clothes," she said.

"Come around to your front porch," Carlie said. "We want to show you something."

What else could she do? If they were going to do something bad to her, she could always yell for Priscilla.

She followed them to the front of the house. On the porch was a bulky-looking plastic bag.

Carlie reached inside the bag and pulled out a scruffy old fake-fur coat. "We got this idea for the Halloween party," she said. "Isn't this coat terrific?"

She held it up.

So, when had they gotten this idea? Had they stopped for a Bee Theres meeting at McDonald's before they came, a meeting to which she hadn't been invited?

She touched the coat. "What are you going to do with it?"

"Go get your big bear-claw slippers," Ducky said. "We're going to transform you into a Sasquatch. You know—a Bigfoot."

"Those slippers you wore last night gave us the idea," Sunshine said. "Actually, it was Sister Jackson's idea. She said she had this old coat that would make a great Halloween costume, along with your slippers."

Ducky grinned enthusiastically. "My mom's got an old fur hat. With that and this," she said, pointing to the coat, "you'll be the scariest thing at the party. Can't you add yourself to our spook alley room along with the mummy?"

"What we can do," Becca said, "is have the room dark until the kids get in there, then suddenly turn on the light so they'll see you standing there. After they've recovered from that, we can show them the mummy."

"Remember that Halloween party when we were little kids," Carlie said, "and Brother Jorgensen dressed up in the dragon costume from a roadshow and jumped out at us from behind a screen? He breathed smoke and everything. I had nightmares about that for a week."

Marybeth, Becca, Sunshine, and Elena laughed, and Ducky said, "I wish I'd lived here then."

Bonnie remembered that Halloween party. She'd been only about six and had clung to her dad and buried her face against him so she couldn't see the dragon.

"With this costume, you'll be even more scary than Brother Jorgensen was," Becca said.

Bonnie thought about it. The scruffy, dark brown,

fake-fur coat was scary on its own. There were bald patches here and there, making it look as if it had some hideous disease or something. Some of the fur was matted and some was spiky and stiff.

Bonnie looked at the coat, then at the girls.

She'd be scary, all right, dressed in that coat and her bear-claw slippers, with the fur hat on her head. She'd probably give all the kids the fright of their lives. They'd remember her for years, like Carlie remembered Brother Jorgensen.

Wasn't that the reason for throwing a Halloween party, to scare people? So why didn't she want to do it? If she said she didn't want to be Bigfoot, the other girls would probably think she was a wimp and she'd never, never, never make it into the Bee Theres.

Was this more of Nesmut's mischief?

She wished she knew what had happened to Nazli.

She realized suddenly that the other girls were looking expectantly at her. Carlie still held the old coat up for her inspection.

Bonnie hesitated. *Just say you don't want to do it,* she prompted herself.

But she couldn't. Not right now. Not when the other girls seemed to think it was such a great idea.

Or did they have some other motive?

She didn't know what was going on—with the

mummy, with Nazli, or with the Bee Theres. The best thing to do was just go along with what they said and try to figure things out later.

"Okay," Bonnie said. She let Carlie drape the coat over her shoulders.

"Get the slippers," Elena said. "Let's see how you're going to look."

Just then Priscilla stuck her head out an upstairs window. "Bonnie," she yelled. "Sister Jackson's on the phone for you. Something about your service project. She sounds excited, like maybe something's wrong."

Bonnie sighed. Did Nesmut have to get a hundred years' worth of mischief into a single day?

CHAPTER
10

Bonnie shucked off the grungy old fake-fur coat and handed it to Carlie.

"I have to go talk to Sister Jackson," she said. "Can you come in?" Her question was meant for all of the girls.

Carlie looked at the others. "Well, my mom's coming back any minute to pick us up. She just had to get some groceries. We'll wait out here." She gave the old coat back to Bonnie. "Keep it at your house, since it will be part of your costume."

Ducky looked a little worried. "Maybe we'd better go in until Bonnie finds out what Sister Jackson is calling about. Maybe we can help in some way. Your mom will honk when she gets here, Carlie."

The other girls agreed that they should go in.

Bonnie was grateful. It was almost as if she were

part of the Bee Theres club and they were going to "be there" for her.

Gingerly carrying the old coat, she opened the door. She hoped the house looked okay. What if Halden had left his weight-lifting equipment all over the living room? What if Priscilla had shed her school clothes across the floor, the way she often did? What if Sport had barfed on the carpet?

But the other girls all had brothers and sisters, and animals, too. They knew that families could be really embarrassing sometimes.

Besides, the important thing was to find out what Sister Jackson was concerned about.

Bonnie hurried to the hall phone. "Hello," she said as she picked up the receiver.

"Bonnie? This is Sister Jackson."

Bonnie wasn't sure what to say. It seemed a waste of time to say, "How are you," if this was an emergency.

"This is Bonnie," she said.

Dumb. Sister Jackson already knew who it was.

Sport came wandering into the hallway from the kitchen. This time he greeted the girls with wags of his tail since he saw that Bonnie had brought them in. But when he spotted the ugly old coat on Bonnie's arm, he backed away, barking. The hair on his shoulders stood up.

That coat was so ugly that it scared even the dog.

Bonnie could barely hear Sister Jackson because of the barking. "Shut up!" she yelled. It was something she normally didn't say, even to the dog.

"What?" Sister Jackson sounded startled.

Suddenly Sport lunged toward the mangy old coat and buried his teeth in its hem. Snarling, he yanked and pulled at it.

Bonnie tried to lift the coat higher so Sport couldn't reach it, but he hung on, even after his front feet left the floor. Ducky grabbed him from behind, trying to separate him from the coat. He wouldn't let go. His teeth stayed embedded in the hem. He shook his head from side to side, apparently determined to kill the coat. All the while, he growled and snarled.

"I didn't mean you," Bonnie said to Sister Jackson. Her voice jiggled as Sport shook the coat. "My dog is—"

"What?" Sister Jackson asked again. "I can't hear you, Bonnie. Are you all right? What's happening?"

"Let go," Sunshine yelled at Sport, and Becca hollered, "He's going to tear it!"

"I'm all right," Bonnie yelled, trying to be heard over Sport's growls and the shouts of the girls. "It's my dog. He's just . . ." She couldn't tell Sister Jackson that Sport was murdering her coat, could she?

"We're just planning something for Halloween,"

she shouted. Her feet skidded across the polished wood floor as Sport continued to yank on the coat.

"Well, the sound effects are great," Sister Jackson shouted back. "What's making your dog bark like that?"

If she only knew!

But surely she didn't still wear that old coat. Perfect Sister Jackson? No way.

And it was a good thing, because the rotting material did rip, as Becca had predicted. The whole thing came apart, and Sport, now back on his feet, trotted happily away to the kitchen, carrying a trailing strip of fake fur in his mouth.

Becca and Sunshine scurried after him, trying to coax the material from him.

Sunshine was saying, "Oh, no. This is as bad as when my dog chewed up the cloth for our bridesmaids' dresses for Pamela's wedding."

Bonnie had heard about that disaster. But she'd been to the wedding of their previous teacher, and she had seen what a miracle the girls had pulled off with what was left of the cloth.

Carlie took what was left of the coat from Bonnie and held it up. "Oh, boy," she said. Ducky, Elena, and Marybeth came over to examine it.

"Wow," Elena whispered. "Even Bigfoot wouldn't be caught dead wearing it now."

"Bonnie?" Sister Jackson said. "Still there?"

"Still here."

"I received a call from Sister Wyndam," Sister Jackson said. Bonnie drooped. Milford had probably complained about her trespassing last night.

"Her grandson—his name's Milford—is going into the hospital tomorrow. He's having some kind of biopsy or something," Sister Jackson said. "He wants to see you."

"Really?" Bonnie was glad this wasn't a complaint, but she was alarmed at the thought of a biopsy. Wasn't that what doctors did when they suspected somebody might have cancer?

She was sorry now that she'd had bad thoughts about Milford.

"Why does he want to see me?" she asked.

"Well, I'm not sure," Sister Jackson said. "I gathered from what Sister Wyndam said that you've already met Milford."

"Yes." Bonnie didn't explain.

"Can you go over there this afternoon?" Sister Jackson asked. "I told Sister Wyndam you'd be going to the Mutual activity tonight. She seemed to think it was important that you come over now. Do you have time?"

"I think so." Bonnie eyed the shredded coat. Had

it been Sport who had ripped the scrap of cloth off the mummy, too?

No. He couldn't have left it hanging on a bush. But why hadn't he at least barked when the mummy was in the backyard? Surely a mummy should have scared him as much as that old fake-fur coat did.

A car's horn honked out front. "That's my mom," Carlie said. "Can we help, Bonnie?"

Bonnie put a hand over the phone mouthpiece. "Do you think your mom could drop me off at Sister Wyndam's? I'll walk home after I'm finished there."

"Sure," Carlie said, and Bonnie told Sister Jackson she would leave immediately.

Becca and Sunshine came back from the kitchen with the strip of fake fur that Sport had torn from the coat.

"Maybe we can sew it all back together," Sunshine suggested.

It would require another miracle, one that Bonnie hoped they couldn't pull off. She didn't want to be a Sasquatch. She didn't want to scare the little kids so they'd have nightmares for years.

Before saying good-bye to Sister Jackson, she said, "The other girls brought your old fur coat over here. When do you want it back?"

"I don't," Sister Jackson said. "When you're through with it, drop it in the garbage can."

So miracles could still happen!

Bonnie yelled up the stairs to Priscilla that she was going to Sister Wyndam's. Then, dropping the remains of the old coat into the garbage, she joined the other girls in the car.

She would decide later what to do about the mummy and Nesmut and how to impress the Bee Theres and all the other things she had to worry about.

Milford didn't seem all that happy to see her when she got to Sister Wyndam's house. He was sitting on a couch in the living room, his right leg propped up on a footstool. He seemed to be watching TV—sort of. Sister Wyndam hovered nearby.

"I was hoping you'd bring your big feet with you," Milford complained.

"I did." Bonnie made a gesture toward her ski-length appendages.

"I mean your Bigfoot big feet." Milford looked down. "Wow, you've got the biggest feet I've ever seen on a girl," he said with admiration.

"Millie," Sister Wyndam said, "that's not very nice."

"Don't call me Millie, Grandma," Milford said.

"It's okay," Bonnie said. She looked at Milford. "Why did you want me to wear my Bigfoot slippers?"

Milford shrugged. "I dunno. They just seemed kind of nice. Soft and, like, comfortable."

"Did you want to wear them?" Bonnie asked.

He grinned. "Maybe I just wanted to see you."

Well, Bonnie thought. If she ever got into the Bee Theres club and the other girls began talking about the guys they liked and who liked them, she could say there was a guy who liked her too. She wouldn't have to mention that he was only nine.

"Would you like me to read to you?" Bonnie wasn't sure what to say to a nine-year-old guy who liked her.

"Maybe I'd rather just talk," he said.

"Okay." Bonnie started to sit down beside him.

"I want to go out on the patio," he said. "Get my wheelchair and help me into it."

"Millie," Sister Wyndam said, "you could at least say *please*."

"Don't call me Millie, Grandma," Milford repeated. Looking at Bonnie, he said, "Please."

While Bonnie got the wheelchair and took him outside, she thought about Milford. Did she like him or just feel sorry for him? He seemed to know how to get what he wanted from people—even if it meant being bossy.

But when he grinned, she couldn't be mad at him.

After they were settled on the patio, she said, "Why did you ask me to come over here?"

"Because of last night," he said.

"Last night? You mean you want me to replay being caught in your trap?" Maybe she should leave while she could. She had no idea what the kid had in mind.

Milford shook his head. "I didn't know anybody would get caught in my trap. I just set it up to see if I could still do it." He made a vague motion toward his legs, which Bonnie interpreted to mean that he couldn't do a lot of things the way he used to.

"I wanted you to come because you weren't afraid last night," he continued. "Because you didn't screech for help and make a big fuss like most people would have done."

She decided not to tell him that she didn't yell for help because she didn't want anybody else to see what an idiot she was.

They sat silently for a moment. Then Milford blurted, "I wish I was like you."

"Like me?" Bonnie was bewildered. But then she understood.

Milford was afraid. And why shouldn't he be? She didn't know why he was here in this gloomy old house with his grandma instead of with his parents, or what had happened to his legs, or how his life in general was. But she did know that he was facing something really big and scary tomorrow.

Should she talk about fear? She should at least tell him that she certainly wasn't anybody he should admire, that she was afraid of a zillion things, including a ghostly mummy that appeared in her backyard.

But right now he seemed to need someone who wasn't afraid.

Should she come right out and ask him what he was afraid of? No, she decided. She didn't want to make him feel worse.

"Speaking of fear," she said, "you should have seen our dog just before I came over here. He doesn't see too well anymore, and he thought an old fake-fur coat was some really fearsome animal."

She told him all about how Sport had done battle with the coat, ending up with the dog trotting triumphantly off to the kitchen with the scrap of his kill dangling from his mouth.

Milford laughed hard as she told the story. "I wish I could have seen it," he said. "Did he really think the coat was something to be afraid of?"

"I can't see into his dim little brain," Bonnie said, "but he sure acted afraid."

"It was all in his own mind," Milford said. "The coat really wasn't anything that could hurt him."

"A phantom fear," Bonnie said. She wasn't sure

where that phrase had come from, except that she'd been thinking so much about the Phantom Fair.

Milford seemed to like her description. "A phantom fear," he said. He was silent for a long couple of minutes, then said, "Do you think I should be afraid of tomorrow?"

Bonnie wished he hadn't asked that. "What do you think?"

"I could die," Milford said.

Bonnie wondered if that might be true.

"Maybe they'll take my leg off," Milford said. Then he flashed Bonnie a quick grin. "But maybe that's a phantom fear."

"I hope so," she said.

Milford's face sobered. "They're going to cut into my leg, no matter what." He rubbed a spot on his leg. "I've got something growing on it. They have to cut it to find out why. It's going to hurt. I know because I've had other operations."

That part wasn't a phantom fear. Things like that did hurt.

Bonnie waited for him to say more about what was wrong with him, but he didn't. Instead, he said, "I wish I could take my teddy bear with me."

"Why can't you?"

"They'd think I'm a baby." He rubbed his hand

111

across his face. "Will you come to see me when I get home from the hospital?"

"Of course I will," Bonnie assured him.

"I'll show you my scars," he said, as if surely she couldn't resist an invitation like that.

Before she left, Bonnie wheeled Milford back inside and got him settled again on the sofa.

"He'll be coming home the next day, if things go well," Sister Wyndam said. "Maybe you can come over and help me put up my Halloween yard decorations tomorrow, Bonnie. My land, getting ready for Millie, here, I've just left it until the last minute. You'd like that, wouldn't you, Millie? Having all the skeletons and witches and black cats and ghost lights up to welcome you home?"

Milford turned his head away, but not before Bonnie saw the look on his face. It was as if the thoughts of the Halloween stuff frightened him.

And this time he didn't even bother to say, "Don't call me Millie."

Sister Wyndam followed Bonnie to the front porch. "Thanks for coming. It did Millie a whole lot of good. Looks healthy enough, doesn't he? But he's got this stuff going on inside, and his mama's dead and his daddy can't take care of him right now. Has to live here with an old lady like me from now on, I guess."

"He's lucky to have you, Sister Wyndam," Bonnie said. She had changed her opinion of Sister Wyndam. Never again would she call her "The Witch of Whipple Street."

Sister Wyndam nodded. "Maybe so. He sure needs somebody. His life's not going to be any bed of roses even if this biopsy turns out okay." She smiled at Bonnie and said, "Thanks again for coming."

Bonnie hurried toward home. Compared to what Milford had to face, she had nothing but phantom fears to worry about.

CHAPTER
11

Part of the Mutual activity that night was the meeting to coordinate plans for the spook alley. The class chairmen were to describe briefly what they'd be doing so there wouldn't be any duplication.

Bonnie didn't feel prepared to report on the Beehives. What had they decided, after all? Or maybe it was up to her to make the final decision about what they were to do. She didn't know. What a disaster she'd been as chairman!

The priests' class started off. "We're going to do Dracula's blood bank," their chairman reported. "We're all dressing in black, and we'll have a sign that says, 'Choose your own vampire,' and another that says, 'Come right in. No waiting.'"

"Brother Allen made fake teeth for all of us," another guy reported. "With fangs."

Brother Allen was a dentist who said his favorite holiday was Halloween. He and his wife and kids always showed up at the Halloween parties with some kind of fake teeth.

The guys, of course, would love having fangs and dressing up in gross, scary, black costumes.

Sunshine, who was sitting next to Bonnie, nudged her. "Have you decided what we're going to do?" she whispered. "You can't be a Sasquatch now that the coat is ruined."

Bonnie wished she could look mysterious the way Nazli did. She gave Sunshine a little smile.

"Did Nazli get a mummy for us?" Sunshine went on. "How about the Grossery? Are we going to do that?"

"Maybe," Bonnie said as if she were hanging onto some great secret until just the right time to reveal it. She couldn't say for sure whether they'd have a mummy. Nesmut couldn't be counted on to cooperate. What if she made trouble for *everybody?* Surely they shouldn't let her loose in a place like the church.

On the other hand, maybe they couldn't stop her from being there.

Bonnie turned her thoughts away from that. She would have to talk to Nazli again—if she ever turned up, which Bonnie was sure she would—and see if she could come that night. Nazli would have to be responsible for whatever Nesmut did.

No, when you came right down to it, Bonnie was responsible for whatever happened.

It made her shrivel up inside to think about it. Why had she let herself get involved in this in the first place?

The Laurel class chairman was reporting. "We're all going to be skeletons," she said. "We're painting bones on old T-shirts and jeans with fluorescent paint so we'll glow in the dark."

That would really be scary, all those glowing skeletons in a dark room. Bonnie wished she had thought of something like that. It was simple and would be fairly easy to do.

The chairman of the teachers' class reported next. "We're going to have a Grossery store," he said, "with a sign that says, 'Lettuce turnip your stomach.'"

"Hey!" Marybeth hissed in Bonnie's ear. "Isn't that one of the things we were going to do?"

"I guess we can't, now," Bonnie whispered back.

"Well, what *are* we going to do?" Marybeth asked.

Bonnie just smiled again.

The Mia Maid chairman didn't say much. "We're going to have some headless bodies that carry their heads under their arms." She rolled her eyes. "You'll have to wait until the party to see how we're going to do it."

One of the guys said, "I'm not going *near* those girls," and everybody laughed.

The younger Scouts were antsy, waiting for their turn to report. Augie Krump was their chairman, and he said, "We're going to have this tunnel into a pyramid, and when you go inside you'll meet a mummy. We're going to make stink bombs and we'll say that's what a mummy smells like after three thousand years."

The rest of the Scouts snickered, and most of the other kids laughed too. But the Beehive girls all looked at Bonnie.

"I thought *we* were going to have a mummy," Marybeth whispered. "They're stealing our idea. Wasn't Nazli going to get one for us?"

"I guess not." Bonnie remembered the rustling in the bougainvillea bushes at school the day she and Nazli had talked about getting a mummy. Now she knew for sure who had been there in the bushes. Trent MacAfee. He was the only one of the Scouts who went to that school. No wonder his ears had turned red every time she looked at him. They turned red out of guilt.

She turned around to see where Trent was sitting and caught him looking at her. He swiveled his head away when he saw her gazing at him, and his ears burned brightly.

It was bad enough that he'd passed the mummy idea on to the Scouts, but did they have to add a stink bomb?

Well, maybe they'd get more than they bargained for. She'd see if Nazli could arrange to have Nesmut transfer all her troublemaking to the Scouts.

She had another thought. Could Trent have dressed up and appeared as a mummy in her back-yard? But then why would Nazli make up all that stuff about a mummy named Nesmut?

She realized that the other kids were all looking at her. It was her turn to report.

So what was she going to say?

She stood up. She cleared her throat. For some reason she thought of Milford and the way he'd looked when Sister Wyndam had said they'd have all her skeletons and tombstones and other Halloween stuff put up in her yard to greet him when he got home from the hospital.

"The Beehive class," Bonnie began. She stopped. Not looking at the other Beehive girls, she said, "The Beehive class promises not to duplicate anybody else's ideas."

She sat down.

118

Somebody said, "Hey, that's not fair. You have to tell us what you're going to do."

But Sister LeFevre, who was conducting the meeting, said, "All we're doing is making sure we'll have no duplications. The Beehives know what everybody else is doing, and they promise not to duplicate. So that's enough. That's the advantage of being last to report." A couple more kids groaned, but the meeting was clearly over as far as Sister LeFevre was concerned. Everyone filed out of the room.

Sunshine patted Bonnie on the back. "You did good. Now whatever we do will be a surprise to everybody."

Bonnie couldn't help but think it was going to be a surprise to her too.

"You've got some other ideas, haven't you, Bonnie?" Becca asked anxiously.

"Oh," Bonnie said, "sure. I just—well, now that we know what everyone else is doing, I can pick something really different for our room. Something creative, you know?"

"It'll be great," Marybeth said. "Call us as soon as you can to let us know what you want us to do."

On the way to school the next day Bonnie remembered that she hadn't ever called Nazli's house to see if she had gotten home safely after she disappeared from Bonnie's yard. She'd meant to do that, but then so many things had happened that she'd forgotten. Some friend she was.

If Nazli wasn't at school, Bonnie would absolutely die. What if she'd truly disappeared?

But Nazli was there in her seat when the bell rang.

Bonnie wrote her a note, "How did you vanish into thin air yesterday?" then added a dozen question marks.

Folding the note, she printed Nazli's name on it and passed it down her row while Mrs. Fisher was calling the role.

It had to go by Trent MacAfee, and Bonnie was sure he was going to read it before passing it on because he looked at her guiltily, his ears reddening.

He *should* feel guilty, the little rat, after stealing their idea the way he had.

But eventually he sent the note on its way without opening it.

When Nazli received it, she read it and scribbled something in reply, then started it back on its way to Bonnie. Mrs. Fisher had finished calling the roll by then, and as usual her eyes were everywhere. She spotted the note right away and confiscated it.

There was a rule about note passing. The rule said that any note intercepted by the teacher was to be read aloud.

Bonnie's palms felt sweaty. There wasn't anything incriminating in that note, but it was scary to be caught doing something that was forbidden.

"Hmmmm," Mrs. Fisher said as she looked at the note. "Verrrrry interesting." She looked up at the class. "Want to know what it says?"

"Yes!" everybody yelled.

Mrs. Fisher folded the note. "Then I guess I won't read it."

Amid the groans that followed, she looked at Nazli and said, "How *did* you vanish into thin air yesterday?"

Nazli looked a little pale. "Ancient Egyptian secret," she said.

The other kids laughed.

When Mrs. Fisher dropped the note into the wastebasket, Bonnie thought it was over. But then Mrs. Fisher said, "She'll tell you at lunchtime, Bonnie. And I think the two of you better stay here and tell me, too. I don't want anybody vanishing in thin air from my classroom."

Before the class could break out with comments, she said sternly, "Now, everybody take out your literature books."

Even teachers wore scary faces sometimes. Maybe, Bonnie thought, she and the other Beehives should have a room full of teachers for their spook alley entry. That should be scary enough, at least for all the school kids.

But that wasn't fair. Mrs. Fisher was just trying to maintain class discipline.

That was exactly what Mrs. Fisher said when Bonnie and Nazli stayed behind after the other kids were excused for lunch. "Note passing can be disruptive," she added. "It isn't anything major. But don't do it again." She gave them a little smile. "Now, for goodness' sake, go somewhere and find out about this thin-air business."

Bonnie and Nazli hurried off gratefully to the outdoor lunch area. Other kids watched them, and some called out comments about vanishing into thin air or about being kept in.

Nazli was wearing a thin gold band around her head that day, like a sweatband. She had a snake bracelet around her upper arm, and on a chain around her neck she wore a gold pendant with picture figures on it. Other than that, she was dressed like any of the other kids, with a long-sleeved green shirt and black jeans. She didn't look quite as foreign as she sometimes did.

Bonnie was a little relieved that Nazli looked seminormal, since they were walking together. She was ashamed of herself for always feeling that way. What was she afraid of? Did it matter what Nazli looked like? Nazli was her friend, she reminded herself for the umpteenth time.

When they were seated at the end of one of the outdoor tables, Bonnie said, "Okay, tell me. How did you get out of my yard yesterday without anybody seeing you?"

Nazli smiled. "I already told you. It's an ancient Egyptian secret."

So Nazli was going to be mysterious. Bonnie didn't push it. Instead she asked, "But why did you go?"

Nazli took a big bite out of her peanut-butter sandwich and chewed silently for a moment. Then she said, "I was afraid."

"Afraid?" Bonnie almost choked on her own sandwich. "Afraid of what? Not afraid of Sunshine and Becca and those other girls. Some of them were right here in this school last year. You know them. And the others weren't going to bite you or anything."

Nazli gazed off into the distance, then looked back at Bonnie. "They're all so . . . so . . ." She seemed to be hunting for the right word. Finally she said, "They're all so put together. I mean, they always look so great and they're smart and they do the right things and other kids like them."

What she was saying was exactly the way Bonnie herself had felt about Sunshine and Becca and the others. Still felt about them, in fact. She was afraid of them too. What were they going to do when they realized she had zip, zilch, zero in mind for their spook alley room?

Nazli put a hand up to twist the snake bracelet around her upper arm. "They think I'm weird."

Wasn't that what Bonnie had felt all along? That the other Beehive girls must think she was weird, with her big feet and her disaster hair and the awkward things she did?

And wasn't that why Bonnie was a little embarrassed to be seen with Nazli—because she was weird?

"You *are* weird," she said, not believing the words were coming out of her mouth. But then she said again, "You *are* weird, Nazli, and I'm weird too."

What if everybody in the world was afraid of what everybody else might think of them, for one reason or another?

"Phantom fear," Bonnie said. "That's all it is. Phantom fear."

"How'd you suddenly get so smart?" Nazli asked.

"From my vast experience in my long, twelve-year-old life," Bonnie said, and they both giggled.

Trent MacAfee was in Bonnie's line of vision at a nearby table. He must have heard them giggling because he looked over at them. His ears reddening, he picked up his lunch bag and slunk away toward the playing field.

Guilty, guilty, guilty.

"Nazli," Bonnie said, "remember the day we heard the rustle in the bushes when we were talking about mummies?" She told Nazli all about how Trent must have heard and then gone on to tell the idea to the Scouts.

Nazli's eyebrows went up. "But that was our idea!"

"Well," Bonnie said, "do you think you could just pass Nesmut along to the Scouts so she'll leave me alone? I'm tired of her hanging around, causing trouble."

Nazli shoved what was left of her sandwich into her lunch bag. "Has Nesmut caused you trouble?" she asked.

"Yes," Bonnie said. "And I'm afraid of her."

"Phantom fear," Nazli said.

Bonnie looked questions at her.

"Did you really believe all that stuff I said about mummies?" Nazli asked.

"Nazli!" Bonnie said. "You mean Nesmut is just a big fib? And all that stuff about calling up a mummy?" She felt her face grow hot with annoyance. "Yes, I believed it. You're so . . ." Now she was the one who was hunting for a word. "You're so mysterious sometimes. You make me believe you know things that I don't."

125

"I'm sorry, Bonnie." Nazli looked worried. "I told you I do things for effect."

"But why?"

Nazli looked off toward the playing field where most of the kids had gone to run off some energy before going back to class. "At least people notice me that way, even if they don't like me."

Bonnie was really ticked off at Nazli for making up all that stuff about Nesmut. But all she said was, "I think you and I are twins. I thought *I* was the only person who worried about nobody liking me."

Nazli looked upset. "I'm sorry I lied to you about the mummy, Bonnie. I didn't think it would get to be such a big thing. I've got a mummy costume and I thought maybe I could just let you borrow it for your spook alley. Do you still want it?"

Bonnie shook her head. "I already told you the Scouts are doing a mummy room. I don't need it any-more."

So Nazli had a mummy costume. Had she been the mummy in the backyard?

But she'd already said she hadn't been the one.

It didn't matter. The mummy hadn't come last night. Bonnie was pretty sure it wouldn't be appear-ing again.

The bell rang, ending lunchtime. Bonnie and

Nazli didn't talk to each other as they headed back to their classroom. It felt kind of awkward.

So Nesmut had caused trouble even though she wasn't real. Bonnie couldn't help but wonder if she and Nazli were still friends.

She was still wondering after school.

The mummy had been real, even though Nesmut wasn't. Not real as in being an ancient Egyptian or anything, but it *had* appeared in her backyard for two nights in a row. Maybe it hadn't caused the problems she'd been having, but it had scared her and she didn't like it.

Why did people want to scare people? Weren't there enough scary things around already without people purposely adding more?

She remembered the look on Milford's face and the way he'd turned his head away when Sister Wyndam had said she and Bonnie would put up all the scary stuff on her lawn to welcome him home from the hospital.

He didn't need any more scary stuff. There were already enough scary things in his life.

There was one thing she could do.

That afternoon when she went to Sister Wyndam's house, the first thing she said was, "What would you think of putting up Christmas lights to welcome Milford home instead of the Halloween stuff?"

CHAPTER
12

Sister Wyndam looked surprised. "Christmas lights? At Halloween? My stars, everybody'd think I've gone around the bend, Bonnie."

Should she tell Sister Wyndam how scared Milford was? She didn't want Sister Wyndam to think she was blaming her for not realizing it. On the other hand, this was important.

"Christmas lights are happy," she said.

"Yes." Sister Wyndam was quiet for a moment. Then she said, "Did you know that for a while we were afraid he might die?"

Bonnie swallowed. "So, how is he? What did the doctors find out?"

Sister Wyndam's face relaxed into a happy smile. "He's going to be all right. The growth on his leg—it was benign. He's going to be just fine, at least for now."

Benign. That meant that it was harmless.

Bonnie hung on to that bit of good news.

Sister Wyndam seemed to be thinking. "Christmas lights," she said. "That seems like a real good idea. Why, I'm such a dunce I was going to put up all that stuff that would remind him. Skeletons and tombstones. One glimpse of something like that and he'd probably take a notion to go all sick again."

"Everybody loves your decorations," Bonnie said tactfully. "We all look forward to seeing them."

"But maybe Millie wouldn't. Not this year."

"Not this year," Bonnie agreed. "Maybe next year. When he's better."

"A dunce," Sister Wyndam said. "That's what I am. Can you imagine? Tombstones! My old house is gloomy enough without tombstones!"

"We won't put them up," Bonnie reminded her.

"We'll use my little twinkle lights that go on and off."

"Perfect," Bonnie said.

"Stars, maybe? I've got stars."

"Stars would be good."

"But no Santa Claus."

"No Santa Claus."

Sister Wyndam nodded. "Around the bend, that

would be. But the other Christmas things. They'd make Millie feel happy. He'll know we're glad as all outdoors that he's going to be well again."

"He'll know we're so glad that we put up twinkles and stars to celebrate," Bonnie said.

"Better than skeletons and tombstones, when you're already scared."

"A whole lot better." Bonnie smiled.

Sister Wyndam smiled back. "We'll do it for Millie. Christmas twinkles and stars."

Bonnie wanted to say, "Don't call him Millie," but she figured she'd accomplished enough already. She'd let the Millie thing pass for now.

It took Bonnie and Sister Wyndam the rest of the afternoon to put all the strings of brightly colored lights and the shining stars up in the trees.

But it was all worth it the next afternoon when Bonnie went with Sister Wyndam to the hospital to bring Milford home. He seemed a little pale as they approached the house, but his face turned on as bright as the twinkles when he saw the joyously lit yard.

"It's like Christmas," he marveled. He gazed around as Sister Wyndam stopped the car in the driveway, and his freckles glowed as bright as the lights. "Is this a present for me?"

"It's for all of us," Sister Wyndam said. "And

you're the best present I ever got, Millie. And you're going to be all right."

"Wow," Milford said. He turned toward Sister Wyndam, looking a little worried. "But what about your Halloween stuff, Grandma? Won't everybody be coming around to see your Halloween things?"

"Well, don't you think they'll love to see all these Christmas things instead?" Sister Wyndam said. "Only a dunce would put up witches and black cats when she's as happy as I am that you're okay."

Bonnie was glad she hadn't mentioned the skeletons and tombstones.

"But aren't people going to think you've gone crazy, Grandma?" Milford asked. "I mean, Christmas in October?"

Sister Wyndam shrugged. "Who cares? I'd do anything for you, Millie."

"*Anything*, Grandma?"

"Anything!"

Milford grinned. "Then don't call me Millie."

Before she went home, Bonnie asked where Milford's teddy bear was and brought it to him. She felt good. Things had worked out okay for him.

And Bonnie felt like she had succeeded at *something*, anyway. Everything else in her life seemed like a bed of quicksand into which her self-esteem and her future were slowly sinking.

Unless she figured out in a hurry what the Beehives would do for the spook alley, their room wasn't going to measure up to the other classes' rooms. She thought about it all the way home.

The fantasy she'd had about doing something really spectacular so the other Beehive girls would be eager to have her in their Bee Theres club was never going to be anything *but* a fantasy. Losing the box of frozen Snickers bars, the prize for the most imaginative spook alley room, was no big deal. But even that would have helped her impress the other girls.

She was glad she'd never told them about the mummy in her backyard.

Which reminded her of that twit Trent. He'd stolen the mummy idea, and Bonnie felt sure he was also the one who had been dressing up to try to frighten her.

Had he borrowed Nazli's mummy costume?

Had she loaned it to him?

Bonnie couldn't help but feel a little scared about her friendship with Nazli. It couldn't have ended, could it?

She needed something comforting. She could put on her Bigfoot slippers. But she needed more than that. It was milk and cookies time.

She found cookies in the red-apple cookie jar and poured herself a glass of milk. If she hadn't grown too old for such things, she would have gotten her old teddy bear to hold while she ate.

Sport came over to the table to beg, and when she gave him a piece of cookie, he reached up to lick her face in gratitude and then lay down close to her feet.

Maybe the world was a scary place for an old dog like him, too.

It was then that she got the idea about what the Beehive class could do for their room in the spook alley.

The mummy appeared in Bonnie's backyard again that night. And again it beckoned to her, urging her to come out, or to follow it, or whatever.

She didn't care anymore, now that she knew who it was.

She flung open her bedroom window and yelled, "Trent MacAfee, why don't you go home and grow up?"

Slamming the window, she yanked down the shade and went to bed.

Halden asked about the noise the next morning.

"I heard you yelling at Trent MacAfee last night," he said. "Were you dreaming about him?"

"Are you out of your skull?" Bonnie said. "He was there in the backyard in his dumb mummy costume. I just told him to go home."

The whole family stared at her. It was Saturday, the day Mom cooked bacon and eggs for everybody and they all ate breakfast together.

"A mummy?" Dad said. "In *our* backyard?"

He said it as if mummies might appear in everybody else's backyard, but surely not in his.

"Trent MacAfee," Bonnie corrected him. "*Dressed* as a mummy."

"Poor little guy probably got lost on his way to a Halloween party," Halden said.

"Maybe we should call the police," Priscilla said, "and ask if anybody has lost their mummy."

Bonnie sighed. They were teasing her, as usual. And once they found out what she was planning for the Beehives' spook alley room, things would probably be even worse. She would always be the Little Sister, fair game to be teased.

That was all right. She was going to go through with it anyway.

She'd have to call all the other class members that morning to tell them they needed to have a meeting. Would they suggest McDonald's? Not likely. That was strictly reserved for the Bee Theres.

Glumly she watched Mom arrange bacon strips around the fried eggs on a platter.

As she did every Saturday, Mom worried aloud. "I should serve you whole grains and fruit instead of all this fat," she said. "I'm clogging up your arteries, not to mention all the calories involved."

And as he did every Saturday, Halden said, "We need all this fat, Mom, to grease our way into the coming week."

Halden seemed a lot more like his old self now than he had when he'd first received his mission call in the mail.

Mom frowned. "I was talking to Ducky's mother the other day. She's really into health foods. Serves her family whole grains and fruit for breakfast."

"Wait'll after the Halloween sugar overload, Mom," Halden said. "Then I'll be gone on my mission and you can health-food everybody else out of their minds."

He looked at Bonnie. "Speaking of Halloween, how is your spook alley project coming along? Are you using any of my fantastic and unsurpassed ideas? I sure gave you enough."

Bonnie shook her head. "Some of the other classes chose them before I did."

"You should have laid claim to all that great stuff right away. So what's left for your class to do?"

Bonnie really wished she could tell him. But he would laugh and so would Priscilla, and maybe even Mom and Dad too.

"Come to the party and find out," she said.

Swallowing the last of her bacon and eggs, she headed for the telephone.

But before calling the other Beehives, she punched in Nazli's number. She missed her friend. This was one thing she could do something about.

Nazli's mother answered. She had an accent that Bonnie liked.

"Nazli gone shopping," she said when Bonnie asked for her. "She feeling very bad."

"You mean she's sick?"

"Feeling bad because she scare you," Nazli's mother said. "She say Nesmut come back from mummy to haunt you. Nazli, she have beeg imagination. You theenk she ees weird-out?"

Bonnie laughed. "Sure, but that's okay. Maybe she'd like to come to our Halloween party tonight. Why don't you come, too, Mrs. Farraj? Grown-ups enjoy it as much as the kids."

"Oh, no," Nazli's mother said. "No, no. I not speak so good. People not like me."

Bonnie was always surprised when grown-ups worried about the same things that kids did. When she was little, she'd always thought they knew everything and were totally sure of themselves.

But she was finding out that they were scared too.

"People would love you," Bonnie said. "We'll talk about it later. Please tell Nazli I called."

136

"You good friend," Nazli's mom said. "Nazli weel be glad you call. She feel bad."

Bonnie thanked her and hung up.

It was time to call Becca and Carlie and Ducky and Elena and Marybeth and Sunshine. She couldn't put it off any longer.

She thought of Milford again as she began punching in numbers. She thought of how relieved he had been that he didn't have to face all those skeletons and tombstones, how happy he was about the cheerful Christmas lights.

Her heart thudded as she listened to the phone ring. She was more frightened of presenting her idea to the other girls than she'd been of the mummy or of anything else for a long time.

They were going to think that *she* was a weird-out. A lame-o.

They were going to think she'd definitely gone around the bend.

CHAPTER
13

That night Bonnie had her mom drop her off at the church early so she could help decorate the Beehives' spook alley room.

There was already a huge computer-printout sign set up on the front lawn that said, "Welcome to the Phantom Fair." A ghost dangled from a tree near the sign, and a jack-o-lantern scowled from atop a stone wall.

The whole place was alive with activity, including the parking lot. Brother and Sister Allen were busy building a crumbling little shack surrounded by a sagging picket fence at the end of their minivan. Little Trunk-or-Treaters would have to come through a squeaky gate and into the shack to get their goodies, and no doubt Brother and Sister Allen would be inside in some kind of scary costumes. Last year they'd been Gomez and Morticia, the parents from the "Addams Family."

Other cars sported witches roosting on their roofs or skeletons seated at their steering wheels. All their owners were ready to hand out treats after the kids had eaten and had gone through the spook alley.

Inside the building, the Primary presidency and teachers were cooking hot dogs and chili in the kitchen, and the Young Men and Young Women leaders were setting up long tables in the cultural hall.

Clutching the bulging bags that held her bear-claw slippers and the other things she'd agreed to bring, Bonnie went past the tables to the long corridor of classrooms where the spook alley would be. The parking lot had been scary enough, but the corridor was worse. She shrank back from fake spider webs, complete with enormous black spiders. Cardboard tombstones were taped all along the walls, and a buzzard fixed an angry red eye on her from up near the ceiling.

Moans and shrieks came from one of the rooms, which probably meant the older guys were preparing their Dracula blood bank. Bonnie hoped the shrieks came from a tape, not from early-arriving victims.

She peeked into the Mia Maids' room to see how they were doing their headless bodies. It was all done with sheets. One girl would sit with her head hidden behind the drapes of a sheet, and another girl would stick her head out from under the first girl's arm. It was a scary room.

Bonnie's stomach did nervous flip-flops as she walked along the hallway. The doors of all the other rooms were decorated with twisted black crepe paper or snarling monster heads or dangling fake snakes (she *hoped* they were fake), so it was something of a jolt to come to the Beehive room and see a fuzzy teddy bear taped to the door. Underneath it was the sign Carlie had made: "COOKIES AND COMFORT. WE WELCOME YOU, NO MATTER *WHAT* YOU ARE."

Dumb, dumb, dumb. Bonnie suddenly wished she could run back home and hide. Everybody was going to laugh when they saw the wimpy Beehive room. Maybe she would be laughed out of the Young Women entirely. Maybe out of the whole ward. This was Halloween, the night for ghosts and goblins and other scary things. Nobody took it seriously. Why did she think anybody, even the little kids, would go for a room full of fuzzy, cheerful, comforting things?

She should have known from the reaction of the other Beehive girls when she called them that it wasn't a good idea. It wasn't that they refused to do it or anything like that. But when they'd been at the meeting at Bonnie's house, Becca had asked, "Won't the kids be disappointed?" And mild little Carlie had said, "Maybe we could have something jump out at people from the teddy bears. You know—something scary."

But in the end they'd all gone along with Bonnie's idea, probably because there wasn't time to think up anything else that hadn't already been spoken for by the other classes.

Taking a deep breath, Bonnie opened the door and went into the room. Ducky, Marybeth, and Elena were inside. They'd already put up a whole wall of brick-and-board shelves. On the shelves were dozens of teddy bears. Big bears and little bears. Brown bears and black ones and white. Even a purple bear looked down from a high shelf.

A whole wall of friendly, happy bear faces.

"Wow," Bonnie said. "Where'd you get so many?"

"I brought my whole collection," Marybeth said. "And then Ducky and I went to a bunch of garage sales and bought all we could find for 15 or 20 cents each. Elena and Carlie and Sunshine were going to see how many they could borrow from friends at school and stuff."

"Aren't they sweet?" Ducky said. She reached out and hugged one of the biggest bears, one with long, soft, brown fake fur.

But was "sweet" really okay for Halloween?

Wouldn't it have been better to have those shelves stocked with bugs and black cats and maggotty bones?

Bonnie had to keep thinking of Milford and the way his face had lit up when he saw the bright, welcoming Christmas lights in Sister Wyndam's yard. And how he'd hugged his scruffy old teddy bear to his chest now that the horrors of the hospital were over. Even so, his life wasn't going to be any bed of roses, as Sister Wyndam said, but at least it had been bright and safe and comforting on the night he came home.

She looked around the room. "Who's bringing the Christmas lights? Did we forget to assign them to somebody?"

"Don't have a cow," Marybeth said. "Carlie said she'd bring a box of white twinkle lights. We'll string them around the room as soon as she gets here."

So what else needed to be done? Somebody had brought a couple of rocking chairs and set them next to a small fake fireplace in which glowed a fake fire. There was a braided rug in shades of brown in between.

The classroom table stood by the window. Bonnie dug into the bags she'd brought and fished out a soft brown tablecloth. She spread it over the table, then set out several brown pottery plates to hold the cookies she and the other girls had baked.

She was filling a gold glass vase with autumn-colored leaves when Trent MacAfee stuck his head in the door.

"Stink alert," he said. "We're testing our stink bomb, so don't be surprised if you sniff something that smells like a thousand rotting mummies."

He looked briefly at each of the girls, and when he saw Bonnie his ears reddened as they'd done each time he'd looked at her during the past several days.

Ducky threw the bear she was holding at Trent. "You keep your stink to yourselves," she said. "We don't want even a whiff of it in here."

"Better get yourselves a fan, then," Trent said. He held the teddy bear at arm's length, examining it. "Is this the scariest you can get? Want to borrow a mummy?"

That was too much for Bonnie. "So you can swipe it from us?" she said. "So you can steal it away and use it in your stupid pyramid?"

Trent squinted at her. "Huh?" he said.

"I know you stole our idea," she said. "Mine and Nazli's."

"What idea?" Trent seemed honestly puzzled.

"You heard us talking about mummies," Bonnie

said. "That day at school by the bougainvillea bush. You were listening to us."

Trent's face bunched up. He seemed to be trying to remember.

"Oh," he said. "*That* day. You and Cleopatra."

"You heard us," Bonnie said. "You took our idea. You were spying on us." She wasn't sure of that part, but she might as well say it.

Trent shook his head so hard his hair bounced. "I wasn't spying. I put my T-shirt on backwards that morning, and the label was itching my neck. So I stopped behind the bush to switch it. Then you and Nazli were there and I didn't want to come out until you went."

When Bonnie continued to stare at him, he added, "I didn't even pay any attention to what you were saying."

Could he be telling the truth?

"Didn't you steal our mummy idea and tell it to the other Scouts?" Bonnie asked.

Trent looked surprised. "Are you kidding? Do you think those other guys would listen to anything I said? I'm the newest guy in the troop. Besides," he went on, "those guys have been planning a mummy's pyramid for a whole year."

"Well then, who . . . ?" Bonnie stopped, reluctant

144

to talk more about the mummy in front of the other girls. They already thought she was goofy.

Who could it be, if it wasn't Trent? Could it be Nazli?

Bonnie slitted her eyes at Trent. "If you didn't steal our idea, why do you look so guilty every time you see me?"

Trent's ears got so red they were almost purple. "Well, gosh, Bonnie. I mean, gosh." He shuffled his feet. "You know. I mean . . . I gotta go back. I'll find you a fan to get rid of the stink."

Bonnie watched him go. She'd thought she had everything figured out. But now she was more mystified than ever.

Marybeth, Ducky, and Elena were giggling. "He likes you," Elena said. "That's why his ears get red."

Liked her? A guy liked her? *Trent* liked her? Big feet and all?

She didn't have time to protest such a ridiculous idea because Sunshine, Becca, and Carlie arrived just then with even more teddy bears plus big Tupperware containers full of cookies and grocery bags holding gallon jugs of milk. Everybody was busy for a while putting cookies on plates and pouring milk into small paper cups.

"Maybe we should just pour a few," Bonnie said.

"We'd better fill a lot," Sunshine said. "The little

kids are almost finished eating their hot dogs. They'll be here soon."

Bonnie didn't say anything. It would probably all go to waste. Probably no one would even come into their room. She would be in disgrace.

Screams echoed down the corridor, which meant the kids had started through the spook alley. There was just time for the Beehive girls to get into their costumes. None of them were scary. Carlie, Becca, Ducky, Elena, Marybeth, and Sunshine wore ethnic clothes that they'd used for an international day at the junior high. Bonnie wore her big bear-claw slippers that Milford had said looked soft and comforting. The little kids who came in would know that the sign really meant what it said: "We welcome you, no matter *what* you are."

Trent came with a fan, which he set up to blow the smells from the Scouts' mummies out of the open window.

"Thanks," Bonnie said as he plugged it in. It was still incredible to her to think that maybe Trent *liked* her. He wasn't so bad looking, actually. Nicer than some of the other Scouts.

His ears glowed when she spoke to him, and he ran off without saying anything.

It wasn't long before small goblins and ghosts and ghouls began arriving at the door of the Beehives' room. They peered in, checking it out. Larger shapes, dressed as witches or Frankenstein's monsters or Draculas, hovered over them, urging them to go in. *Parents,* Bonnie concluded, *or older brothers and sisters.*

"Is this a scary room?" a small girl asked. She held tightly to the hand of the tall pirate behind her.

Sunshine went over and knelt in front of her. "Does it look scary?"

The girl shook her head. "But all those other rooms scared me."

Sunshine took her free hand and led her inside. "Come and meet our teddy bears," she said.

The small girl allowed herself to be taken to the wall of teddy bears. "Come in, Sharlene," she called over her shoulder to a friend. "You don't have to cover your eyes here."

Then suddenly the kids were inside the room, some tumbling over one another getting to the shelf of teddy bears. Others went right for the cookies and milk. Some of the younger ones consented to leave their parents long enough to be rocked by Ducky or Elena.

Ducky whispered stories into small ears. Elena sang lullabies.

One little boy didn't want to go after Elena had rocked him. He made his dad promise to let him eat five treats that very night before he would leave her

147

lap. "One more song," he pleaded before he left. "It's scary out there." He pointed toward the corridor.

A small girl dressed as Pocahontas and her smaller brother, who wore a pig costume labeled "Porkahontas," wanted to take all the teddy bears home. "They keep the bad dreams away," the girl said.

"Your teddy bear at home will do that, won't it?" her mother said. The little girl nodded and took her small brother's hand. They looked back over their shoulders at the wall of teddy bears as they left.

Bigger kids came in and sat down on the rug in front of the fake fireplace. Sunshine and Becca passed cookies to them, and Elena sang them a Mexican song, asking them to join in the chorus.

Some of the kids wanted to try on Bonnie's Bigfoot slippers and asked where she got them.

"This is the best room of all," whispered a little boy as he left, clutching two cookies in his hand.

Then the Phantom Fair was over. The last child left the Bear Room, as they called it. It had been a huge success, and Bonnie was happy, except for the fact that Nazli hadn't shown up.

The Beehives didn't win the box of frozen Snickers bars. The Scouts got the most votes for their Stinky Mummy Room.

The Beehives' Bear Room came in second.

"It's all right," Marybeth said as the girls were cleaning up afterwards. "We'll get plenty of calories at our Bee Theres meeting at McDonald's Monday after school." She looked at Bonnie. "You're coming, aren't you, Bon?"

Bonnie stared at her. "Am I a Bee There?"

Was this the way it happened? After a person had hoped so hard to be worthy of getting into the club, shouldn't there be a few trumpets blowing or something? After she had wondered and practically worried herself sick, was it as simple as just being told she was in?

"Of course you're a Bee There," Sunshine said. "Why wouldn't you be?"

"Well, I thought . . ." They probably weren't interested in what she thought. "Is it because our room turned out so good? Is that why I got in?"

The other girls looked puzzled.

"I haven't been invited to go to McDonald's with you before," Bonnie blurted. "I thought I wasn't part of your club."

Ducky, who was shoving teddy bears into boxes, tossed one at Bonnie. "Listen, girl," she said. "*None* of us have been to McDonald's for a whole month. *That's* why you weren't invited."

Bonnie hugged the teddy bear close to her chest. "I thought it was because of my big feet or something.

I thought you'd never invite Bigfoot into the Bee Theres."

"Oh, wow," Elena said. "If we kept people out for reasons like that, none of us would be a Bee There. Who's the skinniest broomstick in Pasadena?" She spread her arms wide. "Me!"

"Who calls herself Ducky because she was the ugliest duckling for a long time?" Ducky asked.

Becca pointed at her head. "Who has the sickest red hair?"

Carlie laughed. "Nobody's perfect, Bon."

"Except Halden," Bonnie said.

All the girls laughed.

"All missionaries think they have to be perfect," Sunshine said.

"Bon," Ducky said, "I'll tell you the reason we haven't been to McDonald's. My mom's really into health food and all that stuff. She told us if we'd lay off the Big Macs and fries for a month, she'd pay for a night at the movies for all of us. So we did, but the month's over and now we can go back to our bad habits."

"And to the movie," Carlie added.

"Welcome to the Bee Theres, Bonnie," Becca said.

It wasn't too late to call Nazli when Bonnie got home.

She'd probably been too embarrassed about the Nesmut stuff to come to the party. She'd probably been afraid that Bonnie wouldn't want to see her anymore.

That was one phantom fear Bonnie could do something about. She wanted to tell Nazli, too, that she knew she was the one who'd been appearing as the mummy, but that it was no big deal now.

She had just punched in Nazli's number and heard her say hello when she looked out the window and once more saw the mummy in the backyard.

So it couldn't be Nazli.

She'd said it wasn't her, right from the first.

It wasn't Trent, either.

Who was it, then?

Bonnie's spine felt as frozen as an icicle.

"Nazli," she said quickly, "I can't talk now, but I have a million things to tell you Monday. I'll meet you by the bougainvillea bush."

"Great." Nazli sounded relieved.

Things would be all right between them.

They said good-bye and hung up. Bonnie moved closer to the window so she could see better.

The mummy beckoned to her.

She thought of her talk with Milford when they'd tried to sort out his fears. Some fears were very real, but a lot of others would fade away into nothing when a person took a close look at them.

She was going to take a close look at that mummy, and she hoped it would fade away.

The mummy beckoned again.

This time she went.

CHAPTER
14

Bonnie made Sport go outside with her. She needed his protective company. Maybe she should have told her family about the mummy and asked them to go with her to talk to it. But she had the idea that it would just disappear if anybody except her came out of the house.

Sport didn't count.

Bonnie was so nervous that she tripped over her Bigfoot feet. She felt like a little kid again, outside that big black door of her dreams, the one with the skeleton hanging on it.

Or was it a mummy?

Sport pricked up his ears as they crossed the lawn. Any minute now he'd start barking. He always barked at strangers.

Bonnie's heart thumped and her palms felt slimy.

She told herself she wasn't afraid, but she was. This was an unknown. It might even be a ghost.

Could that be classified as a phantom fear?

Sport still hadn't barked. In fact, he dashed ahead to greet the mummy, his tail wagging and his tongue flopping in and out.

Now, that was really scary. She had *never* seen him act that way with a stranger.

So maybe it wasn't a stranger.

Then Bonnie knew.

Walking up to the mummy, she said, "Hello, Halden."

"How did you know?" His voice was muffled through the folds of the cloth around his face.

"Who else loves Halloween so much that he'd do one more gross thing before he goes off to be Elder Perfect?"

Halden groaned and pulled his head covering off. "Oh, Bon, I'll never make it. I'm afraid I'll be a disaster as a missionary. I've tried to be perfect, but I can't keep it up."

So even Halden had his fears.

"You'll be terrific," Bonnie said.

This was a switch, her reassuring him.

"Maybe you can mastermind a spook alley in Romania," she went on. "Isn't that the country where Transylvania is? You know—Dracula's home territory?"

"I'd better just cool it for a couple of years," Halden said. "But I couldn't resist this last time before I go."

Bonnie smiled. "Let's go back in the house and I'll make us some hot chocolate if you'll answer some questions."

"Fire away."

They started across the lawn, with Sport bouncing along at their heels.

"First question," Bonnie said. "What inspired you to be a mummy?"

Halden looked sheepish. "I overheard you talking to Nazli on the phone the other day about mummies."

Bonnie nodded. "Okay. Question number two: How did you make that scrap of old cloth disappear and then reappear when the Bee Theres were here?"

"Promise you won't be mad?"

Bonnie crossed her heart. "Promise."

"Nazli and I were in cahoots," Halden said. "I called her after I got the idea of dressing up. We cooked up the whole thing. Nesmut, too. We thought we might expand your imagination a little, since you were so worried about the spook alley."

"You didn't answer my question. What about the scrap of cloth?"

"Oh," Halden said, grinning. "I took it off the

bush and called Nazli before Mom and I went downtown to tell her where I hid it. She put it back on the bush just before she disappeared. How's that for a couple of geniuses?"

Bonnie punched him lightly on the arm. "It's a good thing I'm such a kind and forgiving person or I'd send Nesmut after both of you." There was one more thing. "How *did* Nazli disappear from the backyard that night?"

Halden's grin widened. "Ancient Egyptian secret."

Okay. So she didn't have to know everything. She already had plenty to tell the Bee Theres when they met at McDonald's on Monday.

Maybe she could get the secret out of Nazli.

Or maybe she would just let it drop. Life was full of mysteries.

Halden opened the door to the house and held it for her to enter. He'd never done that before. In the old days he would have gone in ahead and then held it shut so she couldn't get in.

Confidently, she walked through the door.

She didn't trip.

She didn't stumble.

She felt like a new person. She'd gone out as Bigfoot, but now she was coming back in as just Bonnie.